THE WAY OF HEAVEN

- a little book -

BY

SARAH A. SHERMAN

"To you, it has been granted the knowledge of the mysteries of the kingdom of God, but to the rest, it is in parables so that seeing they may not see, and hearing they may not understand."

Table of Contents

CHAPTER ONE

A Blessing

"They say the whole universe is already inside us," her breath was light, and she had a kind smile. Her hand reached out and touched the girl's forehead.

"You will be alright, you know. Don't worry. He trusts you, and He knows you in a way no one else will ever know you. He loves you more than anyone can ever love you. He is the way to the Kingdom of Heaven."

Where she had touched the sleeping girl, her skin glittered with golden electrical sparks. Then with a blue flash of light, her presence disappeared from this dimension.

The sleeping girl heard the words and felt them deep within her dreams. She sucked in her breath sharply and curled up tighter, tears in her eyes. Her head disappeared under the covers. The memories of this moment played again in her mind's eye, and suddenly she sat up and looked around her room. The touch of daylight had barely begun to change the color of the night. She could hear the brook outside flowing, the sounds of the morning birds, and the rustle of the leaves in the wind. Her cat, Little, chooses this moment to ram her head against her chin.

She stroked Little, remembering the dream's message. Little began to rumble in a deep, content purr. For a moment, the girl almost forgot the pain she was in. For a moment, hope had dried her eyes. For a moment, she believed she might have a future. She hugged Little at that moment.

This is the moment when time could begin.

You are wanted.

Imagine being born into a world with a family and friends; imagine being surrounded by people who want you. Imagine feeling that your unique gifts had value. That there was something, you and only you could do for the planet and all the souls within. Imagine for a moment you are so valuable and so perfect even right now where you are.

She pressed her knees against her chest and hugged herself, leaning back against the wall. She was on her bed talking to herself. Her experience in this world had been a far cry from feeling wanted, at least with many of the people they say are supposed to want you. When people reject and abandon you in key moments, your soul can often feel a little broken.

"You know," she reminded herself,

"I am the best human mom I will ever have."

Unexpectedly, a fracture of her broken soul appeared, comforted enough not to be hidden. It was in a fluffy stuffed teddy bear suit, almost perfect cuteness, but someone was missing. Where the face should be showing, there was just a hole. An empty, dark hole. A little piece of a person who had shrunken so far away was hidden inside. She scooped up the little bear suit and held it close.

Instantly, a bombardment of waves of loneliness, rejection, and despair filled the space. These emotions usually cause people to reject themselves and run off and do something else, but she held herself, the bear, tighter.

Then a muffled little voice came from the bottom of the little bear suit,

"I wasn't wanted."

She whispered a new truth and a future into the bear's ear, "I love you; you are wanted." She gave the little bear a bigger hug, and then right when she did that, a blood-curling shriek pierced through the dimensions. Behind the little bear suit, the interdimensional heavens above opened, and she could see between the realms. There, in the sky hovering, was an enormous, ominous, dark bird. Its menacing presence brought with it horrible emotional darkness, which cast a thick shadow over the area. The bird snarled, screamed, and said, "My name is Grief!" As it wailed in the darkened sky, it gave out a thunderous screech of death. The bird was suddenly and forcefully torn apart by some unseen force. Ripped in half from its forehead to its tail, it collapsed upon itself like an empty shroud and fell straight down. You could feel all its power and presence sucked into nothing, completely disappearing from this plane of existence.

The air filled with the scent of lemons and roses as soon as the bird had vanished. The darkness was gone, and a rosy glow filled the air. "Suicide," the little girl said matter-of-factly. "They did not want me; they told me to get rid of myself." The bear suit climbed up a little higher on her lap. She fell in love with this little piece of herself in the little bear suit and held herself, the bear, so very tightly. She wanted this little piece so very much.

That act of self-love enabled the beginning of the destruction of a caretaker's curse, the curse of her mother. Some mothers just do not want some of their children, no matter how good and perfect the children are. Her mother's curse had unleashed that horrendous, dark bird and set it on a path to destroy her life since she was young. It had ruled the currents of the air above her and greatly influenced her life. She took over her mother's role that day and held herself,

"You are wanted." She repeated the words of truth again.

"You can stay; I love you. You don't have to feel like you are supposed to go anymore."

"You are very important."

"I love you."

The love and light of Christ, the gift of the Creator, had shown her exactly how she could feel in true love. She smiled, and she felt the love flowing through her hands into this part of herself. The loneliness, rejection, grief, and all despair oozed away like thick oil. A little girl's face popped into the bear suit with bright eyes and a perfect smile. Nose to nose, "I love you," she spoke to herself, and as she did, the bear suit girl smiled a big grin. They hugged again, and the little bear began shining a golden light that grew brighter and brighter. The light surrounded them both and became so bright that she could see nothing else for a moment. Then in an instant, this part of her broken spirit became whole. As it happened, shards of darkness shot out of her body like splinters. Darkness could not exist in the presence of the truth. Such is the power of fearless love; it destroys fear. Love can change everything.

Her face lit up with an innocent smile. She hugged herself tightly and immediately was complete and at peace. She leaned back on her bed, smiling because she always wanted a teddy bear suit.

I can count on you – you are wanted. – Yeshua

Now that she could live, there were thousands of potential futures she could live, but only one was the walk and way of the Master. She needed that way in her life. For many years she had gone along the same path, sometimes even following it backward, finding herself right at the start again. Anyone watching from the outside would see that this path was a circle; she was walking in circles.

If your parents forget to teach you about the basics of life when you are a child, it can be a little hit-

and-miss getting it down correctly later. It was time to stop walking in circles. Maybe it was a good time to wake up.

She hugged herself tightly again.

CHAPTER TWO

You are Not Alone

"*You are not alone.*" The Creator spoke to her as she stood up that morning. Her life was often filled with people, although she felt completely alone most of the time.

There are a lot of people in the world, all different types. Looking into the eyes of people, you can see all sorts of things. Some people shine, and sometimes when you look at certain people, you will see exactly what is in their souls.

When she looked at the person that came to visit her farm this past week, she saw the deep darkness within him. She had the kind of sight that noticed the dark flickers within someone's eyes. He smiled at her as she was looking into his eyes; every word out of his mouth was so positive. She watched him and sensed that his personal practices were not in alignment with the Heavens, even though he claimed they were.

But the words, oh the words. Just like the mythical serpent in the garden that could twist dishonest words so elegantly. That is the way of the demons. They want you to doubt God and disconnect you from the Creator's heart.

Sleeping, she dreamed he was a thief, and he needed to go immediately from the house. The dream deeply stressed her because she was concerned about his welfare, doing the right thing, and not creating offense. But often, true and right acts may not look true or right at times.

Demons get offended when you do not give them what they want to take from you. For many years she had felt bad if she angered the demons. They would just be sinister and do the things that demons do. This was one of the circles she disliked walking in. She knew there was the Way, the Dao, the Path that would be in the light and was the truth. Hanging out with demons, you often just go in circles. Getting nowhere.

Out loud, she spoke to the Creator, "I apologize; I made a mistake. More mistakes than I can seem to count. I have been making friends with and trying to please demons for too many years of my life, consciously and sometimes not. I break all these agreements, known and unknown. God, please help me, change my story, and heal my life. I renounce my poor choices and break any contract I ever made by my words, feelings, or actions with demons in human forms." She thought and added,

"And any demons period ever in general. Thank you in Jesus' name." She prayed out loud. She was very serious. It was serious business.

She was so grateful that the Creator of the heavens and earth listened to children's prayers when they broke contracts and asked for help. One by one, she was remaking her past to create a new future. She thought about the Kingdom of Heaven and wondered how she could experience peace.

Reality shivered, and everything around her quickly dissolved. She was standing in an empty place. In front of her was a huge membrane enclosing a giant living fleshy sack; it seemed to breathe its own haunting as it moved in and out. It was large, almost opaque, and rubbery with veins running through it. It was so thick you could barely see a small person's shadow inside. She sensed a part of her had been held there in a soul tie. She felt the cord restricting, binding her – in front of her, the part of her that was trapped was frantically pushing against the walls trying to escape. "I am alone in here; I am all alone. I am alone here." She could hear a distant voice pleading to escape. She felt so alone so often.

The membrane's walls were firm; they could barely be moved. They were heavy, living walls, and they pressed downwards as she saw the small figure inside trying to escape the membrane. The little person inside pushed upwards with all her might. The membrane pulsated, and the small hands were pushed right back down. She sensed that it knew she felt alone. She shivered. She has been looking for this part of herself for a long time.

Immediately she felt the presence of God with her, "I have been looking for you."

She became one with her soul's fracture inside the membrane. Octopus-like cords bound her here. They were giant and rubbery and felt impossible to escape. The feeling was complete and intense; she was almost fully submerged in it. A feeling was completely foreign to the feeling of inner peace, no wonder she felt unsettled. In her spirit, she kept thanking the Creator. She perceived inside herself that this was what happens when you make an agreement with a person who is a demon, a soul tie. The demon tied their souls together in a very uncool way. Sometimes by not speaking up or staying on the path, you agree to be in a situation like this.

"I renounce this; I do not want this in my life anymore!" She said to the Creator.

She prayed for some time and then just quit pushing the membrane and started thanking the Creator, and the Creator's presence manifested right where she was. She continued using her little voice like a serious warrior and came out of agreement with being all chained up and unable to move freely. She just thanked God and continued to speak about what she no longer wanted and what she did want in her life. She asked the Creator to help set her free. She refused to give up or give in. She knew that she had a lot of parts of herself to find. Her soul had been quite thoroughly broken.

The giant octopus-like cord wrapped around her waist, keeping her stuck there; another tentacle bound her arm and wrist. In her mind's eye, she saw the moment the trauma occurred in her life. Years ago, a person struck her violently on the jaw, a dark arrow had penetrated there, and in that moment of trauma, the cord was created, binding her demonically to her abuser. This part of her was caught deep within the membrane, feeling entirely alone and helpless was still experiencing the trauma over and over every day she had been alive.

She cried out in desperation, "Contracts; I break any contract I had with abusive relationships," she continued confessing and renouncing and declaring change for her life and refused to give into fear. She called on Yeshua, the Christ whose blood created grace and a protective shield that all the warriors in the realms understood. Nothing could overpower it.

Yeshua was the Master in the universal realms; He was the living word that held everything together. Nothing could defeat Him.

The cord around her wrist loosed suddenly, and she was free. She felt this huge restraint come off her. She breathed deeply, part of her feeling like it was the first breathe she had taken in years. She exhaled. Then the cord that had bound her waist and kept her here tightly for years was loosed and let her go. Simultaneously a multitude of healings occurred spiritually and physically. Weights lifted. The presence of God was powerful, and she watched the demon connected to this place cast away with the force of a bullet being shot from a gun.

The hand of the Creator touched existence, and the Creator spoke a blessing over her. "The original timing was returned to my life, and I was exactly where I was supposed to be. Double the good would come from my life." She wept because she had felt she had wasted so much of her life trying to please demons.

Once you have touched it, being in the presence of God is somewhere you will always want to be. No doctor, teacher, medicine, man, or woman can be this kind of love. Bones heal, bruises disappear, sickness leaves, and sanity is restored. Like pure love and light, God knit her together. Every energy line in her body began correcting.

Things reversed and returned to normal. She exhaled. Exhausted, and yet in the restoration of the presence, her energy returned.

Hope manifested. She saw Yeshua had come. His hand reached through the membrane like it did not exist. The fracture healed inside her, and then the membrane completely snapped off her body.

Suddenly, reality shook and shifted again, and she was right back at the farm.

Little the cat was standing there. Staring right at her. Little said to her, "This is how we treat demons." She turned away from the demon man person with her tail in the air and started laughing while she walked away.

There is no negotiation with demons.

Walk away laughing and do not look back.

The girl walked away from the demon man and rethought her whole life. She was not alone. She had confidence in the Creator. She was given a special plan in the presence of the Creator and Yeshua. She was a warrior; she could speak. She could just turn away, laughing, and not let the demon trouble her life. She was not called to comfort demons.

Positive.

Don't look back

Seek the solution

Trust God

With her thoughts and life in a new order, she went like starlight away with great boldness in her actions because she knew the Creator was with her. Because of that, she was not alone. Her being smiled a huge inner smile, and she was filled with joy. She spoke her truth in love, then turned, laughing, and went about her day. Not looking back and not caring once if the demon man person did not agree with what she had to say.

She and Little walked away, smiling, and went about their day. Not looking back.

CHAPTER THREE

The Apricot

Sometimes it can be easy to forget the day before, especially while you are getting better. She was standing in the garden back at her own home, appearing to be admiring this very beautiful arrangement of orchids growing outside. But the truth is, as she stood, she was completely unaware of how impressive the orchids looked and how unique each individual flower was.

She often woke up like this, still sleeping while she was awake.

Her actual seeing eyes had run backward and were paused for a moment in time. Although this time was many years ago, she still remembered every word in the conversation. Unfortunately, in this particular conversation, she had only said three words. The other person had mustered up about 172 of the cruelest things a person could say to her for almost no reason at all.

Her mind decided to count each of the 172 words, completely missing the golden butterfly that flew right by her nose and landed on the delicate blossom of a newly opened orchid's lavender-hued petal. Her mind did not even smell the delicious scent of honey mixed with a raspberry that the orchid gave off, which subtly bathed the air.

Her feet moved in the most absolutely fertile soil; she did not even notice at all. Instead, she counted 22, 23, and 24 as she moved through each of the very dreadful words...

"Serious, is this dragging on for so long? Must we entertain this thought again? Thoughts of never letting go and perplexities and worry, worry, worry. It reflects, you know, in everything you experience. Your love is in a state of limitation. You just hang the past on everyone else you meet. Come on, let's let that go. Isn't it time to experience a new life?"

The apricot had come alive in her hands. She jumped; having forgotten she was holding a piece of fruit in her hands. It had a face, a very round one with bright gold eyes, and it was talking to her. She brushed the hair out of her face and stared, her eye widening as she focused on the fruit. Suddenly it had her attention. This was a rather normal apricot, but the tasteless kind, like the ones you find in the markets of South America. Dusty, picked too early, a little not quite ripe enough to be an enjoyable fruit.

"See! There you go again!" The fruit grew two long legs and stood in her hands, and as she watched, hands grew out of its sides. The fruit pointed at her, one hand becoming a long tangly branch, its fingers a mix of leaves and twigs. "See, you have forgotten to remember to look for the beauty, to celebrate," it said, pointing its twigs right at her face, which she had moved closer just to see if it was real. The apricot eyed her intensely as if sizing her up, both hands now resting where an apricot's hip would be. Its eyes grew larger, and it looked square in her face.

"Boo," it said calmly.

She dropped the piece of fruit like it was a ball of hot coals and ran as fast as she could. Pit pat pit pat pit pat, her feet on the stairs scared her more. She sought safety and crawled beneath her bed and remained as still as possible; her breath was freezing in her chest. She lay there, frozen in fear, and a thousand echoes that wanted to be in her mind were silenced. All she could do was listen, listen, listen, intently for any sign that the apricot may have followed her to her hiding place under the bed.

She thought about what the apricot said, about looking for beauty.

Her thoughts beat inside of her head. "It's true." She told herself, "The apricot knows. Almost everything in my life is not beautiful. I dislike almost everything. I am very sensitive; I know what can happen."

Swiftly, she was knocked back into reality when the greatest softness she had ever known pushed its face against her. She felt soothed instantly as she stared into the golden eyes of the greatest gift ever given her. It was just a little cat, nothing at all like the humans. This little cat was perfect. Her thoughts paused; her fear had gone. She jumped up fast on her bed with the little cat by her side.

Little was no ordinary cat; she spoke to the girl in dreams and told her things. Usually, the girl did not listen, but Little tried anyway. The girl was too focused on trying to make everyone happy: the postman, the mayor, the bellhop, the bullies; she gave and gave and gave; now she was just tired, but Little cat was there by her side.

This cat, Little, was most peculiar to look at; the pattern on her fur was best described as "spotted," like a cow, with the colors of a great white shark, steel and white. Her texture was extraordinary; a luxurious blanket of softness covered the slinky-bodied feline. But most importantly, this particular cat was smart, very smart. She only spoke when it was important, which was not all the time, but she knew how to speak her mind when it was.

The girl held Little, and as the cat began to purr, she thought about what the apricot had said. She concluded that the entire story of her messy past and the how's and whys and whatnots that created this whole mess she found herself in was not the problem. She realized that many things happened to so many people that she may never be able to properly figure out and get the answers she felt she needed. That perhaps was not the 172 words that held her in bondage to her past but her thinking about them again and again and, yes, one more time.

On that note, she became sort of positive about what she could do. Being a broken spirit, she needed to enter her inward kingdom properly and find herself. Every little last bit that was not ok. What truly mattered was what was going on inside.

She knew that the Good Shepard said she needed to see the walls of her kingdom. She had built her walls in sorrow, He said to her. Break down these walls, break down these walls; you belong in the light of Christ. She closed her eyes.

She found herself standing outside a large building. The air was dead silent, and the cement building towered above her. Her eyes stared at its base and watched an empty metallic plastic bag of potato chips ride upon a lone breeze. Struggling to survive, a piece of yellowy green grass pointed upwards. There was a small dandelion plant, but its flower had not yet bloomed and was still in a bud.

The earth around the building had that construction gray, compacted, slightly oily from daily filth, untended, and the kind of dirt that resists growth. Flat gray cement squares formed a path that led to the building's door. Her eyes looked upwards. The sky above it was completely gray. Low gray clouds covered the sky, and not a single sun ray warmed anything here.

The construction was not elegant. Rugged and bland, it reminded her of a long-shuddered factory, but she felt that this building was still in use. It could have been an institution or a manufacturing plant, but it most certainly did not look like it contained heaven.

The paint was just about the same gray-green as the earth and the sky, the same green that colors moldy things. The paint was faded and covered with

31

the compacted dust of the soil that ringed the building. The windows were small and dirty, and one was broken. She could see no light inside.

No light shined down on her; she felt a chill glancing at the building. The door was heavy, thick steel yet twisted as if some unknown force had caused it to bow so she could enter.

In there? She thought. This is the kingdom!

"This is your kingdom," Little, her small gray and white cat, said to her. She rolled her eyes at Little expressing her feelings. It had taken the girl too much time to awaken in her life; she was silent in the observation that this was the kingdom she had created within.

But looking at the bent door again, her emotions quickly offered the 1,000 things she could do instead of opening it. She shook them off, left the outside world behind, and was brave enough to open the door. She twisted the door knob back and forth in her hands to no avail. It did not open. She shook it with all her might. Then holding the handle in her hand, she twisted and threw her entire body weight against the door.

Ughhhhpfff. Her shoulder hurt. She slipped to her knees and rubbed her shoulder. The door definitely did not open. She stood back up and looked again. She needed the Creator of all that is and ever was. The only one she could trust to help her.

Inside her heart, she spoke a silent prayer in spirit and in truth. She connected with her breath – and calmed herself in deep reverence and gratitude. She calmed herself. Her anxious mind quickly reminded her that this was only true for part of her being because her broken soul was scattered throughout this kingdom. She trembled slightly because she sensed part of her was wildly screaming in pain. She breathed out and ignored every thought of the emotions with it, and all the rest of her was completely present in a perfect state of love with the Creator.

Her hand twitched. Her stomach clenched. She breathed in peace and kept moving her heart to be in her silent prayer.

She reminded herself of the way to stay positive:

Positive
Don't look back
Seek the solution
Trust God

This time when she looked at the door, it shimmered; a response to her prayer, the door's core became liquid light and remade itself—filling and recreating its space, turning a luminous shiny, glittery gold. It flooded this world with its light. She reached her hand towards the door, and a beautiful handle of crystal and silver appeared. She could feel the peace and joy when her hand touched it.

She almost smiled, looking down at Little. We must be right on time, she thought. This time, the door opened easily, and together, they walked inside.

She looked at Little as the door closed behind them.

CHAPTER FOUR

The Box of Holding On

Everything shifted as soon as she entered the building. The mental anguish she felt was beyond real. She was bombarded from all sides; dark spirits attacked her. They all wore masks of people she had known; they mocked her heart and said cruel things. The same things she had heard so many years ago.

The masks lit up the room in an amazing flash of chaos. Masks from all different cultures and events from all over the world. Suddenly in front of her face popped a bright yellow, orange, and green Mardi

Gras mask - red eyes glowed within the mask as it was inches from her face. Then it spun upwards as many others joined it in its flight. All at once, they all fell to the floor.

The room was silent, and then a small girl appeared with a broom and began sweeping the masks up into a pile. As she was doing this, one mask began twitching, the others soon followed, and the dance of the masks began again. They fluttered all around the room, then gathered in the middle, dancing about, and then fell to the floor in a little pile.

In the center of the room, the small child sat in front of a large box with her broom lying next to her. When the girl looked up at her, she had faraway eyes, and a gray cloud was around her head. She spoke out loud but almost as if she was just speaking to herself.

"God is mad at me," she said. Tears welled up in her eyes, and the little child began shaking. "I needed to be better. I can't be forgiven. It already happened; God is mad."

Suddenly, all the masks of people she knew appeared again. The girl looked beyond what the little fracture could see. In the background of the room, two dark shadows loomed beyond the rest. They were the darkness that ruled this room. The masks got a little brighter distracting the girl, and their mouths tried to bite her heart. Then they fell to the ground and withered.

A mask near the fractured soul part fell to the floor. She wept. "I did not mean to hurt you," she said to the mask. She took her broom and swept the mask up. The room was dark, spare what light was cast through the door from outside. Looking around, even in the shadowy illumination, you could see that this room was kept very clean.

The fractured girl stood up with the broom and began sweeping up more of the wrinkled masks.

With each, she mentioned the person's name, and one by one, she gently put them into the giant box.

This little broken soul was always chasing her memories. It clouded up her thinking. When she looked at someone new, she dressed them in her memories and would put the old masks on them. All the memories she kept in this room were of the people that were mean to her. She had a good memory; she could remember every word.

So, she cleaned up everything as best as she could, and she put all of these memories in the box. It was a big chest. The kind of chest that was normally filled with blankets or sweaters. She did not make too many friends because her box was already full. She doubted if she could fit another pain in it. She called it her box of holding on to things.

She cracked the box open just a bit so nothing would fall out, and the room filled again with a horrible emotion of knowing no one loved her and she was unforgiven. The things she held onto reinforced her feeling this way.

The girl was a grown-up now and not the hurting part. She did not react as she watched herself go through these motions. Realizing the people were not even in this room, that part of her still cried over. She walked to her broken soul and gathered herself up, looking into the far away eyes and this little part of herself that was dressed in rags sewn together; they were filthy and slightly musky, almost like the memories.

She held the head of her broken soul in her hands, and the gray clouds surrounded them. With great love, she spoke to herself from her very own heart.

"It is ok; it is time to forgive. We can let these memories and people go. We can forgive and be forgiven."

She and the little girl began to weep and say, "I forgive you; I bless you, and I let you go." And little by little, the memories allowed themselves to be unremembered, and by forgiving, they were ready to go.

"You do not have to be scared of forgiving someone. When you do, you see the blessing in what happened, and you will feel better."

"God is not a monster! We created the monster. God forgives us; we can let go." The little soul fragment looked at her, and suddenly a sparkle lit up her eyes; her heart glowed and beat one time. She knew it was the truth.

Then the box suddenly opened, and all the memories flew away in a mixture of little bats and happy birds. Love had saved her again. The last memory flew away, grabbing the gray clouds from around the girl's head with its feet. The fracture looked at her and smiled, and with an electrical snap, the two became one soul again.

Just then, the whoosh of large wings distracted her. An enormous bird entered the room, and a great bright light flooded the area. Raphael, almost as tall as the room itself, stood there. Clothed in heavenly armor and weaponry.

He reached into a sachet on his back. "Try these," Raphael said, handing her a rather spectacular pair of glasses. They became almost invisible as she lifted the small lenses towards her face. Dark scales dropped from her eyes, and the lenses of the glasses shone like liquid silver.

The dark forms in the room could no longer hide. These glasses had a special gift of discernment. Discernment helped her see the truth. Behind the box, the two dark shadows still loomed. She could see them now; they were not gods, and she never needed to agree with them again.

"Torment and Unforgiveness," she called them out by their names. "I see you." The demons' eyes grew wide, and torment slightly shook with fear. "You are not God; You tricked me! I renounce you and any agreements we ever made." "Nooo!" Torment screamed, trying to appear taller. "I renounce you in the name of the Christ Jesus," she repeated. With a shriek, Torment withered away. But Unforgiveness laughed. "Remember what they did to you," she reminded herself. Her mind felt calm because the gray cloud was gone, so she just laughed.

"I am forgiven," she said happily and laughed, throwing up her arms. "Everyone is forgiven!" Little still standing by her side smiled, if a cat could do such a thing. Unforgiven withered away, and then the entire room withered like autumn foliage and blew away. All that remained was a golden key; forgiveness is a key. She realized the quicker one could forgive someone, the less the pain could hurt her.

The mansion shifted in and out of dimensions, then reformed entirely. She looked at Little as they were now sitting outside in a different hallway. The door they had come through was closed firmly behind them and sealed shut. The new key, forgiveness, was added to the keyring that she kept in her pocket.

She reminded herself of the Way to Stay Positive

Don't look back
Seek the solution
Trust God

CHAPTER FIVE

The Shadows and The Sword

Her foot ached, and she wanted to disappear. Slouching, she tried to be as small as possible as she walked down the path. Even as she willed herself to become invisible, she knew she wasn't. Anyone walking past would probably notice her even more because of how awkwardly she tried to look smaller. Pain shot through her foot and broke her concentration as she stumbled over a rock. Feeling defeated and tired, she sat between some bushes on the side of the path.

It was late afternoon, and she could see shadows all around her; in fact, these shadows had been following her all day. They were like dark, heavy balls of air. If air could be a bunch of yarn, that was what they were, all tangled up, heavy, floaty things. Little balls of annoying darkness. As she watched them, she noticed those sharp pokey teeth and mean little eyes would appear and disappear in an instant.

Several ran right in front of her and called her names. They opened their mouths, and their words became black arrows that shot toward her. She did not even have time to talk, and suddenly arrows covered her shirt. "Abandoned, too late, poverty." Each little arrow sunk into her clothes and tried to pin her into their words. Another ball of yarn scuttled past her, and a large arrow whizzed with great velocity. "You are hated," it landed right in the center of her heart. Pzzzzzzt. Another hit her in the leg, "lazy," the arrow spoke as it stung her.

She fell directly backward when that one hit her and lay on the dry ground. Her leg was heavy. The bushes around her completely obscured the sun. In the shadow, she felt frozen and stunned. The arrows played with her mind and emotions. They were convincing her that she had no strength to fight.

Tears welled up in her eyes. She was exhausted. Words that no one else could see or hear unless one could see the in-betweens. She wondered about those that could not see what was really going on. If they knew when they suddenly became tired or wrestled with heavy thoughts, it could be the shadows that were bothering them. She knew that you could never agree with the shadows even if they all attacked you at once. Pssssst. "Trapped." Another arrow hit her feet, and she almost agreed with it. She reached for her sword.

Fumbling beneath her cloak, she found her sword. It was a little machete. She held it tightly in her hand. It was a plastic sword; well, the handle was plastic. Cheaply made and attached to the cheap metal blade with a few screws. The blade was rusted and chipped and was not even steel, certainly not Damascus. With a sigh, she lifted it up and swept it in the air once or twice:

"Shoo, go away. I do not like how you feel." Another arrow penetrated her shirt. "Failure." Her tear could not withstand that feeling and crashed into the ground.

One last time she waved her sword. "I hate you," she said and rolled over. Dropping the sword, she covered her face with her hands. Lying on the ground, she was pressed into the earth. "I hate you," she sobbed. She did not know whom she was talking to at this point - the shadows, herself, or the Creator. She wept harder because it is hard to hate yourself and even harder on your soul to hate the Creator. When you hate someone, you want to hurt them and definitely do not want to be around them, but you can never escape yourself, and the Creator is always there.

She sobbed some more, feeling so very trapped. Pzzzzzt. Another arrow sank into her foot. "Trapped," she heard it whisper as if it wanted to confirm her thoughts. Her sobbing picked up a notch.

Chahahahahaha tachahahwahahahaaa A chatter of unreserved laughter took over the air. Someone was there, and they were laughing. The laughing did not stop but got even louder. Chicitawhahahahahahaha chachahahahahhahaaaaa Once in a while, a deep snort like purr broke up the clamor. Brrrrrpppppppppppaaahahahaha, she lifted her head out of her hands and turned her head just enough to see what was going on.

A medium-sized furry black and white tail swept back and forth as an animal rolled around on the ground flopping around with roaring laughter. Chititichacacacacahahahhahhahhaaaa She pushed herself up into a sitting position and wiped her eyes with her hands that had been muddied in the dirt. The creature's feet were paws, and they waved in the air above its body. It had long nails and squealed and chirped as it rolled around in the path.

Suddenly another one appeared on the path. It sat up on its back paws and eyed the scene in front of her. This was a female badger. To be precise, these badgers were honey badgers, which have the reputation of being the fiercest animals in the animal kingdom. They lived to battle. They had no fear.

She was clothed in full body armor, an impossible kind of armor; it glowed and seemed to be molded to her fur yet moved like the softest silk colored in holographic rose gold color. The female badger had a well-fitting helmet on her head, which glowed faintly with pure light. In her hand was an epic golden sword. Slightly embarrassed, the girl shuffled her feet and kicked her small broken plastic machete deep under a bush and far out of sight.

"Festus, Festus," the female honey badger spoke to the badger rolling about the ground. "Do tell me what you find so funny so I can also arm myself with joy."

A shadow ran in front of her, and an arrow flew toward her. "No weapon formed against me shall prosper." The fur raised on the back of her neck at the same moment as she spoke the word. Her giant sword moving by a power that was not her own, carved the shadow in half and, in the next moment, moved to deflect the flying arrow. As the arrow fell to the ground, it crumpled up like a dry leaf, powerless.

"Mom, mom, maaaaaaaa." A mini version of the creature ran on all fours into the clearing. It, too, had armor on, just like the mothers. The creature ran right up to the girl's feet and raised up on its legs to look at her closer. Then it ran directly under the bush. She had hidden her broken machete. The machete was flung back out from under the bush and landed

51

squarely in front of her feet with a clink. The small badger appeared, crawling out from under the bush. Its eyes glanced over to the chipped machete on the ground, and it fell straight away down and started laughing.

Chihehehehehe techehehwehehehehee. Now two badgers seemed to be laughing at her.

Festus, the largest one of the bunch, sat up and then scurried closer to the girl. In front of her, he rose on his back feet to his full height. His armor was like the female badger's but was colored like the sky on a perfect summer day. He slightly coughed, clearing his throat a bit, steadied himself, and chuckled out some words. "You must be the warrior the King told us about." As soon as he said it, he started chuckling; the chuckling became thunderous guffaws and chirps the badgers make. He fell back over and continued his cachinnation, laughing so hard it seemed the ground shook.

Chahahahahaha   tachahahwahahahaaa   the
female badger joined in with his glee. Three honey
badgers laughing hysterically was quite a scene. She
could not help but smile.

Then it happened. 25 or 30 shadows flew in from
all directions and surrounded the group. The energy
around them was weighted by the darkness the
shadows brought in. Three broke off and targeted the
girl; arrows flew straight at her. The girl screamed
loudly and fell back down on her face.

With a roar, Festus rose up from the dust, and his
lips curled, and his teeth showed fiercely. Then he
laughed. "Shadows?" I thought it was serious. His
laughter was so bold all arrows stopped midair and
fell to the ground, withering like dry leaves. "The joy
of the Lord is my strength." His eye caught the girl's
eyes which were still wet from the tears she cried in
distress, and stared at her, "The joy of the Lord is your
strength too."

As he spoke, the shadows began shaking, and then, as a group, they spun around to retreat. The family of badgers went on the attack. The mother grasped her sword in both hands above her head and arched it slightly; she moved it rapidly down and spun in a half circle and clicked her teeth together. The blade sliced through seven or eight of the dark balls; as it touched them, they emitted horrible shrieks and withered, falling to the ground.

The young badger raised its hand and moved it slowly in front of its body palm, facing the circle. It spoke in an angelic tongue and said, "Satan, get behind me." Instantly, 15 or so of the shadow creatures were cast away into nothingness; they moved as fast as bullets shot from a gun. The young badger's sword floated in the air near her the whole time.

Festus had focused on another target. Above in the sky was a large dark shadow bird. Like a puppeteer, it was controlling the attacks below. "I bind you in the name of Jesus," he said. Three golden bands appeared out of the heavenly realms and clamped down on the bird, caging it tightly. It shrieked hauntingly as it fell to the ground in the middle of the group.

The bird smelled like dead meat and oozed a foul brown substance from holes in its skin. Beneath the shaggy feathers, the skin itself writhed, covered by masses of parasitical worms. Its red eyes stared angrily at the group. It opened its beak wide, and rows of sharp teeth, glistening with poison, lined its sides. It started to speak, and Festus cried,

"Do not speak. Be bound in Jesus' name." Golden bands bound its beak tightly, and the bird shook its head and body, trying to resist.

The remaining dark shadows huddled together, stuck between the badgers. They whimpered. The mother badger quickly dispatched them with her sword. Bits of shadows shriveled up instantly and floated powerless to the ground. "It is finished," she said.

The family stood together. "My name is Graceful," the mother said to the girl as she reached out her hand to lift the girl off the ground. The girl took her hand and stood up. "I am Sarah." The girl introduced herself. Festus and Graceful whispered a prayer over the girl, and as they did, every arrow pulled sharply out of the girl and fell, dehydrated of all life, to the ground. Sarah's energy and health were restored suddenly, and she smiled.

The young badger picked up her machete off the ground and handed it to her. "You do not use this that much, do you? I am not sure what you can fight off with this. Maybe a picnic fork? I use the Word for my sword."

For the word of God is living and active. Sharper than any double-edged sword, it pierces even to dividing soul and spirit, joints, and marrow. It judges the thoughts and intentions of the heart. Nothing in all creation is hidden from God's sight; everything is uncovered and exposed before the eyes of Him to whom we must give account.

Therefore, since we have a great high priest who has passed through the heavens, Jesus the Son of God, let us hold firmly to what we profess. For we do not have a high priest who is unable to sympathize with our weaknesses, but we have one who was tempted in every way but yet was without sin. Let us then approach the throne of grace with confidence so that we may receive mercy and find grace to help us in our time of need.

"Your sword looks like you have been running away from God and using your own strength to fight. That is why it is plastic. God is our father, our mother, our friend, and our master. You can ask Him to help. You need to speak the truth with your mouth and heart and become holy in the eyes of the Lord. If you stand with the shadows, you stand against the

King's truth. You must learn how to fight." Graceful spoke.

"I will not die but live and will proclaim what the Lord has done." Sarah agreed, speaking a proclamation of her belief with her whole heart. As she spoke, the plastic sword moved and caught everyone's attention. It began to shake and vibrate. Its blade broke clear in half. It was completely useless.

'Well, that is a good sign. Possibly a very good sign. Using a dull sword that is plastic can get one killed in the long run." Festus spoke in observation.

"Come," said Graceful. "The sun will set soon; come for a visit, and we will go deeper in prayer this evening."

As they walked together, the small badger was speaking, "Aren't you bored losing battles all the time? Being unhappy seems terribly boring."

CHAPTER SIX

The Badger's House

The badger's house was ancient, made from stacked rocks with vines that climb up the sides; it appeared to have been standing there since the beginning of time. A cobblestone path wound around and meandered back on itself toward the front door. When the girl looked at the stones that made the path closer, she could tell that many of them were not from around here, and some may have been from another world entirely. Between the stones, gems filled the gaps, and the mosaic of timeless rocks and glittering gems laid out before her left the girl mesmerized. Labradorite, malachite, pyrite, smokey quartz crystals, and tiger eye japers guided the path towards the old heavy oak wood door. In any spot that was not glistening with the dazzling stones sprung up wild thyme with tiny bright purple flowers that gently swayed in the breeze.

As she walked, the flowers were crushed slightly beneath her feet, and a gentle scent of thyme followed her steps. Along the sides of the walkway, an endless variety of flowering and colorful plants were growing. The air danced with butterflies, dragonflies, and buzzing bees. You could hear the sound of a creek nearby. The air was filled with the chatter and song of birds. A hummingbird colored a brilliant emerald green with giant wings stopped for a minute to stare at her and then quickly flew back to the flowers.

The home itself was built directly into the base of a rock cliff; large vining white rose bushes almost completely covered up one side of the home. The bush had been trained to grow around the windows in the front of the house. The windows were framed in oak, painted a light brown color. Bright yellow curtains peeked out of the windows. Behind the house, jutting out of the mountain, was a ridgeline of sandstone. The house was abutted by this great Hogsback of rock. The formation was slightly angled, and the home fit under the sandstone overhang snugly. The mountain continued up a few hundred meters above and seemed to be alive with vines.

The young badger ran up the path crunching the rocks beneath her feet. In the front of the house, the entry door was a medium height, about half the size of a human door. It was made from the same color wood as the window frame and was also a triangular shape. As she approached, the door slid wide open, and she ran inside. Emerging from the front door, her cat Little walked out and stood on the porch in front of the house.

"Nice to see you came with friends this time instead of your usual guests." Little said and flicked her tail as if to punctuate her subtle sarcasm as she walked up to the three of them. Little, Festus, and Grace spoke among themselves, greeting each other in badger language. The Girl reached down and picked Little up. Not once pausing to think anything was unusual for her cat to be here in this time and place. Little purred deeply as she walked inside the house.

Inside the door was a small opening, and the area was lit by a small triangle window. It reminded her of a Japanese genkan or an American mudroom, a place to hang your coats and remove your muddy shoes. Right now, it was empty of shoes on the shelves that flanked the wall; just a large vase was there filled with dry umbrellas that possibly were just giant leaves on sticks.

A lone hallway opened up in front of them that had been carved from the earth. Together they entered it. Along its walls were many small round glass bulbs that, at first glance, seemed to be ordinary lamps with candles inside. As she walked by, she realized as she looked closely at one that there was a table and few chairs inside. There, four fireflies had gathered and were drinking some kind of hot drink in small acorn cups. The glow the firefly houses gave off lit the tunnel in a warm, flickering light. The whole hallway seemed to be a small town of fireflies and their social activities.

The walls themselves were smooth and the color of light earth. The ground was earth as well and very clean. Finally, they came to a giant round stone blocking the entry. Festus placed his paw on a depression in the stone, and the stone responded by rolling into the wall and opening the path. They all walked in, and as she passed through the opening, the stone rolled back, settling into place. The stone was almost a meter thick; it must have weighed several tons. Most certainly created by a technology that is unknown today.

Once inside, they stepped into a vast cavern carved intricately out of rock. The far wall went up to the arched ceiling and was set with those oddly cut ancient stones laid with great precision. At its base was a large fireplace where a small fire burned. A large copper kettle was suspended above the fire between two poles. The room had a great sense of warmth and felt safe. A feeling of peace was present in the air. A great ledge surrounded the fireplace where one could sit near the fire and warm up. In front of the fire were earth-colored couches, a low table filled with flowers from in front of the home, and a woven rug made from reeds. Wood was stacked nearby, and a large vase containing unusual-looking metal fire-keeping tools.

An ancient badger was seated on the ledge in front of the fire; she had been tending the kettle. Her black and white fur was now completely silver giving her an aristocratic appearance. She was clothed in the same battle armor as the others, but she was dressed in a silvery white. As the group walked into the room, her face lit up into a smile. She stood up and called, "Dayo, Dayo, everyone has arrived."

A tall badger with the same silver fur stepped out of the hallway near the front room. He had a silver cloak on over his armor and walked with a large staff that seemed to have a star glowing at the top of it. His face broke into a giant smile, and his laughter echoed through the room. Festus, Graceful, Merry welcome home." We have been spending time with Darby Little Finch. I see you found the escaped warrior on the trail." "Welcome, Sarah, you are welcome to our home." My name is Dayo, and this is my wife, Simcha."

Little, at the exact moment, chose to ignore everyone and all the small talk. She went straight away to a pillow in front of the fire, where she curled up and fell asleep. Hugs and introductions were given all around, and everyone sat down to rest on the couches in front of the fire. Simcha poured what she had prepared in the kettle into small mugs carved from stone. Everyone received a cup of gratitude.

The girl lifted her cup to her nose and was delighted by its wonderful floral scent. "Honeysuckle and white rose tea," Simcha said. "Picked from the garden earlier today." "It is good to rest after a long walk."

Oliver and Festus were deeply engaged in a hushed conversation. The young Badger, Merry, had disappeared into the badger's home. Sarah sat on the couch next to Simcha and Grace. Simcha spoke.

"It is good you have come, Sarah; our Lord is calling you back to His fold and calling you to awaken and restore what you lost. There is no time to waste. There is much happening in the world today. Men have created great wealth for themselves, fueled by their love of money. They have set aside true wisdom and bullied people with lies and science that is not in alignment with nature and Mother Earth, whom the Creator made. We are the Guardians of Creation here on this earth, as we have been since the beginning of this world. Tonight, we gather to give thanks to our Creator and pray for our hearts and the leaders on this earth to heal, and we pray for the provision of protection and well-being of our brothers and sisters around the planet.

We are children of the light, and yes, the dark brothers seek to escape this world in a way in which there is no escape, only destruction. For the way to be free is not an outward path but an inward journey. To heal and know one's soul in Christ is the Way of Heaven. If you seek first the Way of heaven, all you need is given unto you.

You, my sister and child of God, have a great grace on the planet. It is an honor to be given the grace and wisdom to repent in this hour. Much of the world is deceived, and we must pray for them."

Festus and Oliver then joined them in the sitting area. From all directions in the house, several small brown house mice gathered around their feet. Listening. Little walked up to the mice, and the largest of the bunch bumped into her as if she were a close friend. Little sat listening, surrounded by all the mice.

Festus spoke.

"The Way of our Lord in prayer is to pray until one sees a result." You must come before God in recognition that you need Him; you must unburden yourself by communicating the things that have burdened you, your mistakes, your shortcomings; if you hide unforgiveness in your heart, you must seek to make peace with those whom you have in against. Go through these things in case one keeps your prayers from going before God. In Jesus, we have the forgiveness of our sins and the release from karmic debt. We have freedom in Christ. Call upon the name of the Lord and be saved.

To get results and to be in the presence of the Creator, we need to heal the kingdom of heaven within us. We need to find the places in your heaven and in the foundation of your life where the energy of your soul has a foothold. Then we can petition the Creator to deliver and heal you. You have been running for years. He will not let you run anymore. You run because you expect Him to punish you. It is the opposite, the true Creator, not the false man-made gods, the wolves who gather souls in false churches; the true Creator is a God of mercy and shows mercy, love, healing, and restoration to those who seek Him.

Some people think the Creator is their puppet, their toy, and deny His name if He doesn't bend to their irreverent prayers and disrespectful asking. The Creator is alive and living and has a plan, hope, and a future for you and all. He wants a relationship with you. Not an empty prayer, not a shallow commitment. He raises up warriors.

There are many beings on this planet, some quite ancient, that would want the truth to be hidden. Some beings were cursed to live off of the dust that man had been cursed to become. In Christ, we are a new creation, old things have passed away, and we have been freed from that curse. We war not against flesh and blood, but things many cannot see in the heavenly realms or warfare are through our communion with our God and walking in the spiritual authority we have been given.

Simcha continued.

"With Christ came many, many gifts. We have been given the spiritual anointing to bind beings that are our enemies, heal the sick and walk in the way of miracles. It is not the way of this fallen world; it is the way of heaven. We are strangers to this world, a royal priesthood, a holy nation passing through and collecting our brothers and sisters to come home within us." She tapped her chest, "Christ lives within me and you, and through Him, we can be one with the Creator. One body, One."

The mice stood upon their hind feet. All the mice wore little white robes. Together they sang in Hebrew:

Psalm 27.

The Lord is my light and my salvation—
　　whom shall I fear?
The Lord is the stronghold of my life—
　　of whom shall I be afraid?
When the wicked advance against me
　　to devour me,
It is my enemies and my foes
　　who will stumble and fall.
Though an army besiege me,
　　my heart will not fear;
Though war break out against me,
　　even then, I will be confident.
One thing I ask from the Lord,

this only do I seek:

That I may dwell in the house of the Lord

all the days of my life,

To gaze on the beauty of the Lord

and to seek him in his temple.

For in the day of trouble

he will keep me safe in his dwelling;

He will hide me in the shelter of his sacred tent

and set me high upon a rock.

Then my head will be exalted

above the enemies who surround me;

At his sacred tent, I will sacrifice with shouts of joy;

I will sing and make music to the Lord.

Hear my voice when I call, Lord;

be merciful to me and answer me.

My heart says of you, "Seek his face!"

Your face, Lord, I will seek.

Do not hide your face from me,

do not turn your servant away in anger;

you have been my helper.

Do not reject me or forsake me,

God, my Savior.

Though my father and mother forsake me,

the Lord will receive me.

Teach me your way, Lord;

lead me in a straight path

because of my oppressors.

Do not turn me over to the desire of my foes,

for false witnesses rise up against me,

spouting malicious accusations.

I remain confident of this:

I will see the goodness of the Lord

in the land of the living.

Wait for the Lord;

be strong and take heart

and wait for the Lord.

As they prayed, the room was filled with an interdimensional living flame; many angels entered the closed space they had just flicked in. The air was charged with joy. The presence of the Creator was in the space.

Dayo spoke in a deep, rubbing voice.

"Let us approach our Creator in prayer. They all took a moment within themselves to connect with the Creator in reverence and supplication." The little mice held their hands together in a prayer position.

"Creator of all that is, Creator of all existence, the Father and Birther of all creation, the one whose breath we breathe, the one who holds the universes in the palm of their hands.

We sing praise and speak gratitude to your name, the name so holy only you can say the truest of your names. We worship you. We thank you for your son, Yeshua, who opened the Way.

We ask for your kingdom to come, your rule, your peace, your will be done here on the planet on earth as it is in heaven.

On this day, we thank you for your provision, for being the provider of all of our needs - food, shelter, water, and air - all of our needs.

We are all transgressors and have made mistakes; please forgive us for every step we took without regard to its impact. That you would forgive us for the times we acted outside of your perfect will. Please heal us from these transgressions. We need you; without you, we are nothing. You are the lifter of our head. The healer of our souls. Heal our brokenness and cast us not away from your presence.

Let your love rule in our hearts so we may forgive others and make that choice always. Letting go of those burdens in our souls.

Let your love protect and guide our hearts so we are not deceived by temptations, vain causes, and things that would take us on a false path. Please, Creator, protect and deliver us from evil; you are our reason for living.

Creator, all is yours, the kingdom's within and without. You're the power and weirder of it, and all the glory in all that is you.

Throughout all times, lands, and eternities.

"It is so. Amen and amen."

Festus spoke:

"The life of a prayer warrior is one of deep communication and time spent with the Creator. It is written that the sins of the one in deep mistakes; the cries are not heard. We, as intercessors, stand in the gap and cry out on behalf of the oppressed, downtrodden and hopeless and proclaim the liberty of Christ.

Then you must learn the word. You must know how to speak the word with faith and declare things that have not come to pass; just like the world was spoken into existence, we who have been created in the image of God can speak things into existence.

People have been deceived into not understanding this power. Look at the prayers and mantras and things people agree with. Music of this day, the movies, the videos. People create contracts with their words and their energy. You have the power to come out of agreement with every curse you have spoken over yourself, every song you have sung, bringing in agreement with lyrics that you do not want to happen in your life. You have the power to renounce these agreements and seek your deliverance. Then you can sharpen your sword and speak the truth in love. You can carry a sword that frees people, changes the world, and can restore hope to people.

Plastic is what they sell today. Discard that broken sword and take up a sword that is your divine inheritance, and discipline yourself to use it every day.

"We will pray for you now, Sarah." Said Simcha.

Dayo held a green glass pitcher in his hands; he lifted it above Sarah's head and poured it out upon her. Olive oil scented by cinnamon, frankincense, and other indiscernible scents covered her head and dripped down upon her. The group of badgers laid their hands upon her praying their words were an angelic tongue. Deep notes sang from within their hearts, bypassing the limits of words. Fire surrounded them, and the Holy Spirit connected their hearts in direct connection with the heart of the Creator. The room, the Universe, and every dimension shook as the supernatural force of the prayer brought restoration, freedom, and healing in minutes.

Deeper and deeper the prayer went. Sarah began weeping as she felt many things in her life free. As a group, they lifted their hands to the heavens and prayed, speaking change to the earth and God hearing the prayers of the broken-hearted. They spoke about futures to come and blessings to be had.

Then a great stillness entered the space.

In the stillness, that place of rest, every burden from their hearts was lifted.

Sarah slept well for the first time in a long while. She reminded herself of the Way to Stay Positive

Don't look back
Seek the solution
Trust God

CHAPTER SEVEN

A Key to the Kingdom

"Wake up, Sarah," Sarah opened her eyes to see Little staring at her face from an inch away. Tap, Tap, Tap. Little's paw tapped her on the forehead. "Let's go see if we can find the dungeon today." Sarah sighed a deep breath thinking how that sounded like a very uninteresting thing to do, but Little was full of plans.

"Where is the dungeon? Let us keep searching, and if we can find it…" Little stood upon her chest fearlessly and peered at her.

Little batted Sarah's nose with her paw and said, "Where do you go? When the kingdom is right inside of you."

As Little's paw touched her nose, they both began to get smaller and smaller, the dimensions folded and bent. Then suddenly, there they were, standing inside the building right in front of an old antique door with a brass keyhole. The girl touched the keys in her pocket. She selected the key of forgiveness and placed it in the keyhole. It fit perfectly, and when she turned it, the lock clicked open, and so did the door.

They entered into a vast, dimly lit foyer with many hallways breaking off from the center. She could see near a dim light in a dusty corridor a door. It was faintly outlined in one of the hallways. It was an unremarkable door, the kind of door that, if you were just too busy, you would walk right past.

It smelled like someone had hoped very hard she would never find the door. The scent of invisibility.

When she touched it, the handle felt very frail and cold. It opened on her first try, and the darkness in the room came to life and sucked her right into the room.

The darkness was so encasing and so complete she could not even tell if Little was near her. In the darkness, you could hear the tears of a small child crying and talking to herself.

"God cursed me," she said. "I was cursed by God," she heard it repeated and then again and again. Immediately the girl came up to her; the little child could barely stand. She felt very frail, so tiny, just about an inch and a half tall, and was so weak. Like it had been a long time since she had water or food. She had just been here alone, sitting in this great darkness. Weeping, the girl was overcome with compassion and held this tiny child in her hand, this fracture of her soul, this teeny piece of her, so near death, so hopeless. The darkness was so complete here.

Then she heard a shuffling noise, and an unfortunate-looking man stepped out of the dark. He reminded her of a magician by the way he moved. He had dark brown curly, unkept hair and a bulbous nose with bad acne. He swept the teeny fracture right out of her hands and held her by her hair. He snarled at her and pushed the girl to the ground laughing. "This is mine!" He said, holding up the fracture; he chuckled in a gross way. His laughter was like dark oil that stains and permeates fabric, a heavy belly laugh that reminds you of evil things. You could hear the snot in his voice when he spoke.

He went and sat down in front of the worn, antique wooden desk that was against a wall dropping the soul fracture in front of him. On the wall above, many wooden shelves, almost to the ceiling, held hundreds of glass bottles of different shapes colors, and sizes, some new and some old. In each one, you could see a little human moving. He selected one of the bottles. It was tall and narrow and was made of brown glass. This one only had a very small skull and a lot of dust in it. He dumped the contents into a small tray on his desk.

The man eyed the soul fracture watching him; she was scrunched forward, holding her knees tightly, and sitting on the desk. He plucked her up by the back of her gray nightshirt. She shook her body to try to free herself, but his grip was strong. He dropped her right inside the bottle and pushed a cork tightly on top. Her hands tried to reach the top of the bottle, but she wasn't tall enough. He turned to the girl on the floor. "You!" He cried, pointing at her. She levitated, then shrunk completely and suddenly was inside the bottle next to the little fracture. She reached out and put her arm around herself.

On the glass wall of the bottle, a memory from her life began to play like a movie. The adult little girl was so frightened she almost felt frozen in time. She struggled to find her balance; her eyes glued to the movie. The woman that appeared on the screen had held all the keys to her universe. She was the woman that brought her into the portals, the dimensions of time. She was screaming at the little girl. It felt so very real. It was her mother.

The little girl had come to believe that this woman just did not love herself; she hated parts of herself and was in a great deal of pain. With her new glasses, she could see evil spirits in the woman's mouth. It wasn't the woman at all; it was a spirit of vodka yelling.

Although the woman was dressed in elegant clothes and drove an expensive car, the woman was not happy; she was bored, in pain, scared, and treating her sadness with alcohol.

In the movie, the woman screamed even louder. She told the little girl how hated she was, how everything was going to fail her, how she would always cause problems, and how no one could love her. She told the little girl because she gave birth to her, it would always be true.

The little girl hid in a quiet room and locked the door. As the sun set and the room grew dark, the woman threw things at the door screaming at the little girl, telling her she had no mommy, she would always be bad with no family. She screamed and screamed at the little girl, then made her voice normal and called the other family members and told them how bad the little girl was, how evil she was.

Inside she never felt very good because the woman that gave her birth never could give her real love. She had always been the scapegoat. When she was little, this was hard because she was always being punished. She and her fracture were having a bit of a struggle watching all this. They moved apart from each other in the bottle.

The big little girl sat there in the bottle in complete shock. She really needed a miracle to survive this. She had been really trying to be a good mom to herself, but sometimes, she realized, she acted a lot like the woman who gave birth to her. She gave herself mean love. When she realized this, and she looked beside her to help her fracture, all she saw was the fracture's nightgown. Somehow the fracture had escaped, but fractures were like that. Part of her was lost again.

The little girl sat motionless in the bottle. When she opened her mouth to speak, she had a new stutter; she was someplace else. Parts of her had gone away again, but she felt all the way broken. She felt very sad, very alone, and very empty. Her thoughts kept trying to be in the movie; she never meant her mother to hate her so much. She had always wanted a family, but she was often alone. She did not know how long she had been in the bottle.

She could feel the heaviness and fear of the lies. She breathed in and breathed out; the oxygen felt like it was disappearing. As she walked inwards, the past tried to move her. She focused on her breath. With each breath, she was able to connect with the Truth of God. She witnessed strongholds being broken.

Chains break, and gifts are returned. But it felt so hard. She would send love and speak truth to her inward parts, but this was a heavy magical stronghold. She called on Christ; she called the blood of Christ.

She watched the man lift up the bottle she was in and begin to paint a magic symbol using the spider's blood on her jar. She realized this was the altar her mother had made for the girl by her words, and it cried out for the little girl's lifeblood. This was the demonic minion's assignment to destroy her life. Suddenly the strength of the Creator welled up within her heart, and she jumped to her feet with all her breath within. She screamed at the top of her lungs.

"I forgive her; I forgive my mother! I bless her and absolve her of any and all karma. I forgive her of any wrongs; I forgive her and bless her from the bottom of my heart!"

The cork flew off the top of her bottle before the symbol could be painted. In shock, the man's fingers loosed around the bottle, and it slipped from its hands and landed on his desk. She covered her head as the glass completely shattered. She crawled out of the broken bits of the bottle that had held her.

Another bottle slipped from the shelves on the desk and fell beside hers. "You can't forgive her. She is a terrible drunk that yells at people!" The man said angrily. His mouth curled into a snarl, and he raised his lip above one side of his teeth. He leaned in close to the little Girl. She, free from the bottle, stood and shouted at him, **"I FORGIVE HER COMPLETELY!"**

Another brown glass bottle, which was slightly bigger and looked like an old pharmaceutical bottle suddenly exploded as if the force of her commitment to what she was saying caused it to break. A wildly drunken woman stood up with a face of anger. Her fingers pointed at the air. She was ready for a fight. A tear dropped from the little girl's eyes as she realized her mother had been fractured as well, and this was the part of her that needed healing. A great light suddenly illuminated the center of the room as a great wind caught the fracture of her mother and whisked it away.

Little was nearby, she had locked eyes with the minion, and he was trembling slightly under her gaze. Her claws clicked the floor as she walked closer, making golden sparks.

The soothing presence of the Great I Am, the God of Moses, the God of Abraham, Moses, and Isaac filled the space, and a giant rushing sound of wind filled the air. A mighty light illuminated everything, and the archangel Gabriel entered the room.

You are blessed by God, Miracle.

The light had illuminated where her soul fracture had hidden. In the middle of the floor, there was a pile of dirty rags. They moved slightly, and a small face peeked out. She had tried to make herself as small as she could.

The minion snarled and tried to move forward but was pushed back into a corner by Little; the angels moved behind Little, hands-on swords. The area was secure.

To overcome this demon, she had to love; she had to love her in pain. She walked forward and sat down on the rags. "It was my mommy!" She cried, "My mommy cursed me!" The fracture was traumatized, but freedom was close. "Shhhhh, shhhh, you are ok, everything is ok; we are here now. No matter what she said, the Creator did not curse you; the Creator is our friend." The sliver wept tears that could never be cried before this moment; her shock had been so complete. "I love my mom," she said, "I love her so much." With big tears, the girl and the fracture's eyes looked at one another and became one, a diamond suspended between them for a moment in the air.

Then she was whole, weeping in the dust and pile of rags, hugging herself and telling the universe how she forgives her mommy. Then the rags rustled, and she could just make out the shape of a unicorn's body next to her in the rising dust. The air shimmered in gold slightly. The regal head of the Unicorn lifted from the rags, and the girl clung to her neck, tears beginning to dry. She recognized this unicorn; it was her favorite Unicorn friend! Her mom has cursed her Unicorn too. Her Unicorn had been missing for so long. Unicorns were the best way to travel in the kingdom. She hugged her Unicorn tightly for some time. They sat on the floor together and regained some strength as they returned to the presence of God.

Bravely, the little girl spoke out loud to all existence, separating herself from any contract or agreement with her birth mother. She said she had become her own mother now and accepted the blessing from the Creator - the father, mother, Creator of all existence had blessed her with LIFE. Thanksgivings were whispered to the Creator.

In the high heavens, dark and ancient fortresses crashed apart and broke as principalities were cast down and powers shattered. The magic curse of her mother broke. The desk and the minion folded up upon themselves until they became a small cube and finally disappeared from this existence. Her Unicorn struggled and then stood up; its body covered in old rags. It pawed the ground, lowering its head in reverence to the Creator, then shook itself, and the rags and dust flew. The body of the unicorn sparkled and began glowing brightly as its beauty was restored.

A flash of light filled the space, and the room transformed into a bright and colorful space in a split second. The girl was dressed in white, her hair long and flowing. She had merged together with her fractured self, healing completely. The weeping in the room and inside of her ceased.

It had taken until this moment in her life to break free from that spell. At this very moment, she knew that nothing could separate her from the love of God.

She was learning never to flee from a fracture of herself again despite how terrible it feels to face yourself. She must boldly meet herself in every pain or misstep because God was there and would transform everything. She could trust God. God would meet her in pain.

She smiled and hung her arms around the Unicorn's neck. This Unicorn was her steed of adventure and helped keep her safe on the path. "I missed you," the Unicorn spoke in its native tongue and told her secret things. She had learned to understand the languages of many of the Creator's creatures. Her tears of fear and sorrow turned to tears of joy, and laughter filled the space. She and Little climbed up and sat upon the Unicorn's back, and the room transformed into a great garden with a beautiful stream. Her smile was gratitude manifested. A crown of butterflies circled her head, and a great grasshopper sat upon her shoulder. This was a Kingdom she felt comfortable in; this was a space where she could be understood. In her heart, she knew she was in the right place.

The Great I Am spoke – *"You are a fighter."*

The finger of God touched her on her forehead, *"I Am with You."*

The Great Spirit whisked them all away.

CHAPTER EIGHT

The Birth

She was with God and standing on a hill. In her hand, she had a great sword; the living word of God's name was etched into it. It was sharper than any two-edged sword known to man, yet she could touch it without being cut. It felt alive in her hand. She knew that when she carried it, the word would penetrate, dividing soul and spirit, joints and marrow, judging thoughts and attitudes of the heart. The sword would never hurt anything or anyone that walked in the truth, the light, the way. But would utterly destroy anything that did not yield to the truth of the Spirit of the living Creator. Nothing could stop it. Darkness shook whenever it was nearby.

The tip of her blade touched the ground behind her. She snapped back into reality as it clicked against a rock, sparks flying. She began to lift up her sword then realities snapped and untwisted. In her mind's eye, she witnessed her rebirth.

She saw a dark giant vulvic cavern carved into a gulley in the earth. She felt her birth mom's energy and her inherited energy. She watched her body forcefully birthed from this cave on the hillside. As she entered the world, earth's womb pushed her out; she had been born under a curse. "You had not wanted it," the curse screamed at her again and again. Then it was over. The earth thrust her out.

"Never return. Never return," she said like a mantra. She turned her back on the one who did not want her and knew that she could never go back. To love herself in that deep mess of pain took all the love she could hold. She was shaken.

"I rebuke the curse of your mom," God said. "She is not your friend." A subtle layer of darkness and rags fell off of her like a filthy garment; the curse was rebuked by the Creator. Her white clothes were lighter.

She was lost in her thoughts…

Memories wanted to pull her in several directions. Guilt, hesitations, loneliness, expectations, what ifs, and whatnot. A feeling of victimhood wanted to stain her, "Why me?" We all have heard how our stories are supposed to be perfect. Everyone wants a mommy and a daddy. Everyone wants to be good.

Then his hand, the Creator's hand, touched the back of her head. "What happened to your head?" The back and side had been deeply broken on the spiritual level, and in that brokenness was a river of tears. God adjusted her head, and she felt her spiritual bones realign as memories of being physically and emotionally hit began fading. She smiled. Like really smiled.

"I will be a father to you, and you shall be My sons and daughters." - Adonai-Tzva'ot

As an adopted child, the Creator welcomed the girl into the household, the family of the one that created all the universes. The curses of generations and bloodlines were rewritten into a peculiar blessing given to a royal priesthood and a holy family after the order of Melchizedek. She had a new family. She had inherited the blessing of Abraham.

As she heard the words spoken and understood the intention, she wept. She fell to her knees, face upon the earth, and cried out in gratitude from the deepest part of her heart. Barely understanding her inheritance, slightly comprehending that she was wanted and, in that seed, that tiny seed of comprehension, a spark of gratitude arose and met the fingerprint that the Creator made in and on her heart, Mercy. Her tears pooled below her face on the ground as she cried out her heart, confessed her shortcomings, and said thank you for accepting me when all have rejected me, and I have hated and neglected and hurt myself.

"I need you," she whispered to the Creator. "I cannot be without you. My every breath is a testament to your love."

Yet to all who did receive Him, to those who believed in His name, He gave the right to become children of God— children born not of natural descent, nor of human decision or a husband's will, but born of God.

Praise be to the God and Father of our Lord Jesus Christ, who has blessed us in the heavenly realms with every spiritual blessing in Christ. For he chose us in him before the creation of the world to be holy and blameless in his sight. In love, He predestined us for adoption to sonship through - Quote of an Ancient Text

Jesus Christ, in accordance with His pleasure and will— to the praise of His glorious grace, which He has freely given us in the One He loves. In Him, we have redemption through His blood, the forgiveness of sins, in accordance with the riches of God's grace that He lavished on us. With all wisdom and understanding, He made known to us the mystery of His will according to His good pleasure, which He purposed in Christ to be put into effect when the times reach their fulfillment—to bring unity to all things in heaven and on earth under Christ.

In Him we were also chosen, having been predestined according to the plan of Him who works out everything in conformity with the purpose of His will, in order that we, who were the first to put our hope in Christ, might be for the praise of His glory.

And you also were included in Christ when you heard the message of truth, the gospel of your salvation. When you believed, you were marked in Him with a seal, the promised Holy Spirit, who is a deposit guaranteeing our inheritance until the redemption of those who are God's possession—to the praise of his glory. Quote, of an Ancient Text

CHAPTER NINE

The Monster

Her work wasn't done yet, the Creator of all that is had just adopted her and completely saved her life, but she had some misconceptions. She could see and feel them. Something wasn't quite perfect. She looked down at the gown she wore, and her finger rubbed on a dark spot. Her smile turned downwards, and her eyes furrowed. This is still stained. Then her heart clenched again, and she knew she was ready to press in. For most of her life, God had been a monster.

The Kingdom of Heaven dwells within us.

Break down the walls of sorrow, break down the walls.

Transform. Break down the walls. Boundaries.

That was the mission.

And clean your room.

Ahhhh, but she wasn't ready for this; she felt an inexplicable fear rise in herself at the thought of cleaning her room. Her broken soul felt intense emotions deeply, and, acting on these emotions, she ran screaming. Her feet hit the ground hard as she dug in with her toes, propelling herself forward. Her hair and her dress followed her, caught on the current of the wind created by her running body. She kept running and shook her head, "No!" She said to herself, "You want to hurt me. You are mad at me. I made a mistake, and I can't be enough." These thoughts pushed hard on her head because they wanted to trap her mind. The healed part of her struggled to be the leader here, but she ran.

The girl was letting her thoughts be influenced by things outside of herself. She was letting them rule her actions. Suddenly she knew she was entrapped. Where was this heaviness coming from? Where was this pain? She was confused. Was it God? God was so angry sometimes; why does He want me to clean MY ROOM?

Just yesterday, everything felt ok. Was this witchcraft enchantment? The thoughts raced, chasing with heavy energy. She raced; she ran. She just needed to be someplace else. But where can one go when you are running from yourself?

As quick as that thought appeared, another thought so much heavier pushed on her head again, trying to enter, and she was more confused. If God was real, why did He not want to help her?

She continued to run from God as best she could. She forgot her battle strategies. She ran some more. Running away from the pain, the confusion, the problems. Suddenly, she completed a circle around the mansion and ran right into where Little was.

She flung herself against a wall. Hands on her knees, chest heaving, gasping for breath. With one hand, she pushed her hair out of her face and looked at Little. Little chose this moment in time to completely ignore her. Instead, she was chewing on a toe on her raised foot.

The girl returned to her own drama. She already felt tired, and she had just woken up. These things made her life very hard to do. This wasn't the first time she ran in circles, getting pounded by thoughts she could not see. Like part of herself was trapped in a dungeon, the thought alone made her cry.

She tried to think straight. She felt the heavy weight pressing her head again. Every time it pressed harder, her thoughts were more out of order, so she stared at her feet. She started crying again just because she forgot to put her shoes on. She was shoeless; it was terrible. She did not even have socks on. She turned and faced the wall in complete misery.

She felt if God was mad at her, she had no real purpose. More tears fell because her hope was lost within her broken soul, and when she cried, she felt she was rarely answered, and these thoughts troubled her.

The tears made her cheeks feel hot and sticky.

She knew that she could not abandon herself here again, and the Creator was always with her, so the partially healed part of herself encouraged herself to find stillness and inner peace.

It sorts of worked, but almost all of her felt like God was angry with her. Part of her was pretty angry too. Who wants a monster for a dad? She had been hiding and running for all her life from God. Do this, she ran, do not do this, and she did it. There was just too much she always did wrong.

The kingdom is inside of me. She reminded herself, touching her heart.

As if on cue, all of her being sucked right inside her heart. Then she was there.

The mansion was alive and beat like her heart. Mansions can be rather large places, with many rooms and little nooks and crannies. Places to hide, places to lounge around in the sunlight, but this room was an empty place; she wasn't sure why she spent so much of her time there.

She started running again, and then she ran faster, "I just need to get there now," she thought out loud.

The room she sought was lodged under a stairwell near the basement. The air down in the basement was never fresh, the light never quite bright enough... It felt a little damp sometimes.

Whoever had painted the basement near the stairs lacked any sort of creativity. It was gray, that standard stale gray that had no hint of a supporting color, like the cement in a parking garage in the city. Like an empty hospital floor or the most lackluster gloomy day etched in smog and pollution. It was the color designed not to be noticed, and she had never noticed it before. She just saw the door she was looking for.

The door behind the stairwell was small and hidden. She pushed it open with both hands, and once inside, she slammed the door tightly shut and fell down in front of it. She would hide here when she felt like she had done something wrong. This was one of those times. She had made this a small refuge. An assortment of books and her laptop lived down in the room under the stairs.

She just wanted to be alone and not be around monsters. Maybe she could read or watch a movie and try to forget. She picked up her keyboard and clicked play on a video. It is funny, though, trying to forget what you want to remember. Maybe there is a better way.

When she had calmed enough, she opened the door to the room under the stairwell just enough so some light would come in. She could barely see the outline of a small bookshelf, the desk, one pillow, and a blanket on the floor. She liked the blanket; large fluffy, and probably had not been washed in years. No one noticed it was missing, though. She supposed no one knew she was here.

But Little, her cat, could always find her everywhere. She was Little, the cat, after all, and she always knew just the right moment to arrive.

Clean your room.

Little was staring at her. She said, "Enjoy your run!"

The girl hit play on another video and did not answer. "The peace you seek is not there. Looking at that which is outside of you to distract you from the pain within is not the solution." Some days Little liked to talk a lot.

"Have you considered that God may not be a monster? If God is your friend, who created the monster?"

Little was so calm and confident that she began to feel very safe. Little was smart, too, so If Little was talking a lot, the words were very important. Her words meant a lot, not like some cats who just liked to talk about food or birds in the yard.

"Caretakers and people in authority represent God to the little children. If you were abused often, you see God as just another abuser." It was getting scary. "The father that tried to kill you creates an energetic power that pretends it is God in the spirit realms. Beating you with eternal torture." Her head hurt. The pressure was still there.

Churches, too, she thought. A fancy church doesn't mean God is there, at least the God who created the Heavens and the Earth. One thing she remembered about reading the Bible is just how well the devil and his human puppets knew the Bible perfectly as well. They could repeat it better than she could. She touched her heart, reminding herself where the kingdom was.

She needed to find that place inside her that still hurt. Little hopped up on her lap and purred. She fell asleep thinking about that.

In her dream, words were written:

The Dao
I am not mad at you.
Every morning, wake up with peace in your heart.

She sat up. As she reached for her pen, her hand shook, and the tears flowed freely. But the words she wrote from the dream would someday become her life.

Her hands shook terribly as she wrote the exact words down. So scared, still broken, it was hard to be excited. The dream held such beauty, grace, and mercy, and it was not how she thought the Creator felt about her. The dream world was still there, and she pressed her eyes tightly closed, stretching her body. She could still feel the dream. She smiled even as she shook deeply inside and out.

Opening her eyes, she pointed at her heart and said, "The Kingdom is here, inside of me." The love of Christ and the golden light surrounded her; she knew The Dao was the way, and Christ was the way. He was her friend. She stepped into the day knowing what she needed to do. She needed to find the next broken part of her and bring that piece of her soul back into alignment with the way.

Many little children may not understand what it is to face monsters every day. Some boys and girls have to do this. It is what they were given, wrong or right. They all have a gift from God, the power to destroy the works of the monsters in their lives. It is the power that Yeshua gave them. There is power in the blood of Yeshua; they could call on mercy. The children have been given the power to destroy the works of the dark one, the deceiver, the one who comes to kill and destroy. She sat up and wore a long white dress and white combat boots.

"The monsters can be terrible things; they thrive in creating fear through their lies. Perfect love casts out fear." She continued to speak to herself. "There is no confusion in perfect love. The monsters tell us there is no way. Having a monster issue is like having a filthy house. You just have to clean it up and make it stay clean by taking care of it."

Ha! It sounds so easy. Clean your room, she thought. She started walking, watching the worlds change around her as she descended within the lower realms seeking a part of herself again to tell the good news. Her unicorn was there and walked alongside her. The tunnels grew darker; along the walls, the dead were in the walls like zombies and completely unconscious. In gray, they writhed, bodies piled on top of one another. Many people lived and died behind these walls. Never waking up in their lifetimes. Deeper and deeper in the tunnels and world she went.

She glowed and sparkled golden blue as she walked. She carried the presence, the vibration, and the breath of the love of the Creator. Everywhere she put her foot down path opened up before her. She had to be pretty brave to do this. She needed courage. Facing what you run from can be pretty intense.

As if on cue, a power came out of nowhere and rammed into her head for no reason. She could see this one. It looked like a giant blackened tendril that was connected to some faraway place. It belted her over the head. A black bird joined it and wildly went back and forth around her life and told her horrible things. It sat down and proclaimed it was the god of her life.

Another tendril smacked hope down in her life. It said the most terrible things. It pushed her hard in the chest and condemned her because she had a bad thought 27 days ago. It shoved her again and showed her how little she had done for the kingdom of God and how she needed to feel more guilty. Suddenly huge chains appeared out of thin air and clamped onto her, "I will destroy everything just because you breathe."

Then, she arrived. In front of her, a humanlike being was also chained. So very thin, almost unrecognizable. Every human part was scrubbed off. It was chained, arms stretched wide. Voices filled this space with unimaginable fears. The force kept cursing her and the chained being.

Her Unicorn moved forward towards the damaged fracture. The entity cut in front of it and raised its hands, and the horn of the Unicorn changed to wood. "You will never change!" The power screamed.

"Too late," the human-like formed whispered," you are too late. I ruined everything already." The girl realized this pitiful creature was part of herself.

This could be the beginning of a very bad day, she thought to herself. She looked at the broken part of her spirit that lived in very bad days. She realized that she was human, and humans make mistakes; that is humanity.

This fracture hurt so bad she tried to erase away her humanity to please an out-of-control power created by a human that wanted to break and control her, and she agreed to it. The girl struggled with the new chains on her wrists, feeling bound as she tried to comfort herself. The chains grew tighter, and then more chains clamped on her feet. Every time she tried to move, she clanked.

Little chose this moment to sit in front of her calmly with great gold eyes staring at her in what appeared to be slight disbelief. "What are you doing?" She asked. "I am experiencing the presence of god" the girl said, jerking at a large chain. "Really, is that so?" Little scoffed. "Not my God," she said and turned and walked over to the humanlike shape and began comforting the fracture of her soul.

Then, it all made sense. The warrior in the little girl suddenly wondered why she would allow this. The girl had been serving a false god, a rather nasty one at that. The girl kept breathing and stilled herself in the midst of the insanity. Because that perfectly described insanity, agreeing to and running from the perfect love of the real God. The one that created everything. Not these terrible imposters and those that worship them.

In her soul, the truth was a brilliant light. The Christ within her heart exploded with light. I AM - the name of God was written in her heart. She spoke, "I renounce this and any false god. I break the power I have been given then in the name of Yeshua."

Click. The chains broke and fell to the ground. She rubbed her wrists and realized that she could never have escaped on her own; she needed the Spirit of the living God within her.

She made it to the center of the room and gathered up the soul splinter who was desperate to erase its humanity. She could feel a faint heartbeat. She shivered. It felt boneless, spineless; you could see within its body as it was almost transparent.

Without a mouth, the humanlike splinter said, "God is here; He doesn't like me. I don't do anything good." As she spoke on the wall in front of her, a small dark spot grew larger and larger, and a tendril came out. It pushed against the girl's head, and as the dark tendril wrapped around, it secured itself with the suction cups on it.

The girl's tears welled up in her own eyes, and her body was shaking now, but she willed herself to be strong, to be love, to be courageous. Now she could see the truth; this spirit was not her friend and certainly not God. She began praying because she needed the real Creator to help her.

As she prayed, the monster pressed in; its control and oppression were felt everywhere. Tendrils shot out of the corners and crevices of the room. She held the eyeless fracture and, in a moment, saw what it saw. Visions cast into the broken soul-stained reality with madness and lies. Across her mind, the demon projected an onslaught of visions of horrible things in the future merged with what it declared was an unforgiven past. "Because of you, I will do this" - the dark power became a huge force and form. He merged with the entity of destruction. "I am your

father. I am your daddy. I am your mother." The liar
lied.

The splinter withered and cried out in confusion,
"I do not know what to do; I try my best every day!"
It screamed with no mouth. The girl held her splinter
close with all the love she had; it was hard to do. She
held the fracture and stared into the no eyes until they
were connected and said, "I love you; I am you."

"God is not a monster. This is a power, energy.
This power is a liar. It is not true. We do not have to
agree with it." She held her broken, scared, shaking
self. "We can clean this room and leave this place. We
do not belong here."

The girl strengthened herself and became a
mother and a father to herself by holding her
fractured inner child and whispering to her the truth.
"We created the monsters. God is different; God is
love and kindness and forgiveness and joy. We made
the monsters. We gave people's monsters power by

believing and agreeing with them. If we are fearful and guilty, we will do things for them. God is not a monster. The monsters are not our God; we do not bow. We can let these monsters go now. We do not need to be afraid anymore. We do not need to be afraid anymore. We are safe."

"Let's say a prayer to the Creator of all that is. In the name of Yeshua, I call upon you, holy Creator. I know you are not a monster. Please destroy this power and cause it to shrivel and dry up. Please heal us and replace this lie with your truth. I renounce any agreement I ever made believing you were a monster. Please forgive me and lead me and restore me to the right way, the way of unconditional kind love. Heal us, have mercy on our souls because we made mistakes."

She continued to pray out loud, protected by the blood of Christ and speaking her new testimony, sitting on the floor with her soul fractured. She was shaking. She could feel a light shining on her back;

the light grew bigger and bigger and warmed her. Monsters were still attacking her from all around, lying to her and saying terrible lies about herself. Her soul felt like breaking again; this trauma had really upset her. She needed help. Trying to put your trust in one who had always seemed like a monster takes a step of faith.

Right then, angels arrived singing, "Glory to the Creator." An angel spoke and said to her, "You are loved, you are accepted as you are, you are more than accepted, you are blessed and special in the Creator's heart." As she turned around and stood in the light, the shakes of guilt subsided. Her ego died. God was not mad at her. The dark power swelled and pressed towards her and then exploded inwards on itself. As if everything within it had never existed. Then the skin on the power fell to the ground like a dry cloth.

The light pierced through the whole room and grew brighter and brighter and brighter. As the light grew more intense, the remaining monsters simply withered in it and disappeared as shadows always do when the light comes on. If you see a monster that wants to enter the house, do not let it enter. This is easy when you are in the perfect love of God.

The room she was in was filled with light, joy, and peace. Like a sudden explosion, every wall broke in the room, and her whole kingdom suddenly became lighter. This part of her broken soul had healed in the flash of glory. The explosion of light expanded and filled her heart. She was sucked into that explosion of light, and instantly, she was returned back to the hill with her Unicorn and Little.

She felt better than she had in a very long time. Understanding what power was. Power was what was created by witchcraft, manipulators, and those who, by their desire to control, made the energetic realms heavy. Christ came to destroy these evil works.

She inhaled the fresh air and touched her head. Upon it, she had a warrior's helmet. The Helmet of Salvation.

CHAPTER TEN

Grasshopper

A bright green grasshopper landed on her shoulder. "What happened to your ears?" He looked into her ear. "Hmmmm, I see. I see the problem." The grasshopper was wearing a lovely plaid vest which was interwoven with colors that looked as fancy as butterfly wings. Underneath it, he had a long sleeve button-up shirt that seemed to be made from tawny wheatgrass. His cufflinks were seeds, perhaps apple seeds.

He reached into his vest pocket, pulled out a golden monocle, and sat it firmly over his eye; it glinted like the sun. Grasping his cane firmly at the top, which was perhaps made from Bubinga wood. The canes were carved in leaves from top to bottom. The tip of which looked rather pointed, and he raised it to her ear. "Hold still a moment," the grasshopper said politely. He could have been an English hopper or an Irish one. His speech was slightly accented from both areas... perhaps he hopped around.

"Ouch!" She said, moving her hand upwards. "Got it." The Grasshopper pulled back his cane which now had a large black string attached to it. He began pulling the string, and the string was tied to bit and bobs, rather large bits and bobs, and as he pulled more, the string got longer, and little big rocks and other oddities all began coming out of her ears.

"That explains a lot. You could not hear a thing with all this rubbish in your ears." He blew into her ears, "Phfffffff!"

"Yessir, that is all clear now." Suddenly she no longer heard all the tormenting voices. All she could hear was what was being said the whole time—so many positive things. "Ha," he laughed heartily. "That is one way to see one's curses transform into blessings!" Monicle back in his pocket, the grasshopper tipped his cap and said, "See you around," and then flew off.

She sat there for a little while listening—the sounds of nature, the beauty of creation, sang its song. Music and peace entered her ears. Her cat head-butted her and interrupted with a rumbling purr.

Little smiled, as only cats can, she had that look of adventure about her, and she said, "Now you have faced the monster's power; it is time to get set free from the minions. Let's go to church."

In her mind's eye, she saw a big fancy church building.

You won't find me in there. God spoke.

In her heart, she knew that was the truth.

Feeling very clear-headed with her new helmet protecting her mind and her ears cleaned out, it became clear she had been seeking God in a variety of kingdoms of cons. She had been conned. She allowed it to happen.

She needed to find that place inside of her that still believed any lies, that was mesmerized by the lies. She had entered the kingdom of cons in great pain, hurting badly as so many often do. She had hoped someone could help, heal, forgive, and absolve her of her guilt and pain. Anyone, just the perfect coach, the perfect words, the perfect prayer, anything, she just wanted to feel better.

God helped her because she was hurting so badly, and she knew what the Creator felt like. Nothing like a con, nothing. God is not fake. God was not out to get her and was cruel. God did not want to torment her for her mistakes.

Watch out for false prophets. They come to you in sheep's clothing, but inwardly they are ferocious wolves. - Ancient Text Quote

Demons are masters of deceit. They are artful cons. It seems they very much like to pretend they are holy, people of the light. The devil knows the Bible like the back of his hand. He tempted Christ with the very words of God, and even with Eve, he just twisted everything around. The enemy comes to steal, kill, and destroy.

Yeshua had some strong words about some church people in His days:

Wolves in Sheep's Clothing
Hypocrites
Showoffs
Blind Guides

Whitewashed Tombs

Murderers

Thieves

Brood of Vipers

Sons of Hell

She wandered through the hallways of the large mansion, thinking about these things and feeling the tensions from them within her soul. How when one is guilty or hurting or struggling with sins, these demons can enter and go on a rampage and set up control in people's life.

In the hallway, she came to a large purple chair. It was velvet and wood with a tall back. Almost plush, almost regal, but it was a bit worn. Little hopped up on her lap and purred. She was an interesting color spotted like a cow but with the colors of a great white shark, gray and white. Her fur was extraordinary cat fur, like a luxurious blanket of softness. Little was smart. She only spoke when it was important, which was not all the time, but she knew how to speak her mind.

Little wasn't overwhelmed by her past either. The girl had looked for help in so many different ways to try to make herself better. As she was thinking these things, the air around her shifted, the golden light she was surrounded with faded, and an eerie neon glow filled the air. Then the music started, and like a pop-out book, the mansion unfolded into a whole new space.

CHAPTER ELEVEN

Pomp

He was a big, big man and even larger on stage. He paraded around huffing and puffing – "Sing louder, sing louder now - bow." He shouted to the congregation in a booming operatic-like voice to people whose salvation hinged on his every word. "YOU need to know I am holy, Hurrah, Hurrah, Hurrah. I am a great prophet Hurrah, Hurrah, Hurrah. The creator of everything made me His PROPHET; I can see everything." He pointed at the many television cameras that were following his every move. Knowing this, his feet danced a little jig, and he waved his hand in the air.

"HOLY I am. I can SEEE RIGHT INTO YOUR SOUL! Glad it is going to heal you tonight. Show GWAD you're glad and send me some money!"

He danced a little shuffle back and forth across the stage. He slid, mesmerizing everyone there. As she looked at all the people in the audience, they reminded her in a subtle way a snake can charm with a flute, moving back and forth to the music. In an instant, she saw they were mesmerized by his magic. They seemed disconnected from reality and were bound by his deceit.

The eyes of one of the members of his staff in a fancy white suit caught her eyes. The eyes shifted, and the pupils became thin like a snake. His mouth opened slightly, and his eyes glowed red while a spilt snake's tongue slithered out between his lips. Meanwhile, the self-proclaimed prophet continued his chanting.

"I fast three days a week on nothing but air. I memorized all the Psalms to protect YOU! I am holy, holy, holy; I am a prophet of Gwad. Now Bow," He boomed. "Bow to God by giving me your dollars. Give me your dollars so I can protect you; it's for the children, you know."

The band dinged some bells, and as if on cue, his robotic crew moved, holding golden buckets. They were all dressed in white, wearing little caps a lot like chefs' hats. They passed around silver buckets to the watching crowd. Pling, plonk, plying pling. The sound of money, wallets, jewelry, checks, everything entering the buckets was faintly reminiscent of some casino in Los Vegas. Pling, pling, chachinggg.

"Your money! Give your money! If you give me your money, Gwad will make you rich. Rich, rich, rich in the kingdom." This man could sing and looked like he was almost tap dancing too.

"Fill the plate to the brim with your dollars, your tithes. I will read your future and shout your fortunes. All the cash in your bank and pockets will do. Don't be greedy with Gwad because he will stop your blessings. I know everything he knows; I do. You must obey me because I am special; I am most holy."

She did not know if there was a more intense purple color than what this man had on. He was encased in yards upon yards of purple silken fabric, like a ball gown for men. Golden thread was woven through it. A large, costly gem-encrusted cross hung around his neck. Just in case you had forgotten how special he was, his clothes were sure to remind you. He pointed to the sky, and his fingers were stacked with platinum and diamonds. "Gwad knows how much is in your bank. He knows if you are greedy. Greed won't get you to heaven. Giving will."

Her eyes rolled back in her head. How did I get in this room again? Oh my, oh my. She shook her heart and head. A tear dripped from her eye. She shook off the feeling of the projected guilt. She wrestled with the spell of God being such a monster. "Money, money, money." His choir had about 15 well-dressed people singing. They swayed back and forth.

"You better not disagree with me." The man shouted, "or Gwad will take your life because I am holy. Anointed to tell your fortunes. Paid to forgive your sins."

She grimaced as she wiped it away, a little harder than normal, almost like she wanted to push it back into her face. Ah, I remember. It took her experiencing a lot of pain and asking for help to even trust a person like this. He told her he was holy, that he was special, that he would help. He was a fake. They are the wolves; they prey upon the hurting.

"No! No! No!" She said, standing up in the purple velvet chair. "You are a LIAR!" She wasn't all the way well yet. Saying these words to such a man took some effort. "LIAR, you are a liar, and you have no control over me."

Baboom! The Choir and its chorus stopped, and the room went silent. The man stopped his dance and turned slowly to look at her. His mouth opened slightly, and a snake's tongue peeked out. His eyes became the eyes of a snake. A spotlight fell upon her, lighting only her in the room. She felt every eye on her as the neon light shined on her skin.

Suddenly he cast a shadow over her as he seemed to vibrate and levitate, his eyes turned red, and his tongue hissed. She realized he was a snake. There wasn't even a man there; he was pure evil. Beneath his robes, a thick large snake tail was where his legs should have been. She could see clearly now the costume he wore. He came towards her, bellowing and hissing.

"How dare you come up against me, you little girl, the root of all evil in the world. I am a holy and otherworldly apostle that is in the highest place of honor here on earth. Heaven and men bow to me." She moved quickly back, away from the snake, and kept her silence. "I will destroy you. You are an ingrate. You never gave me enough money! How dare you refute my efforts in front of my sheep." He licked his lips, and his fangs showed venom glistening on the tip.

"We will destroy you. I work with Gwad, God, God, God, God!" His clothes and the building flashed in pulsating neon effects when he said that. Like all the sin that held Babylon together oozed into this place when he spoke. As if on cue, he turned to his audience, "Put your money in the plate, and I WILL FORGIVE YOU. More, more, more - prove to me you care about God. Show God how much you love Him and give me money!" He slid back and forth across the stage, breaking into a song. Like an enchanted snake, he reversed the game.

"God does my every will because I am perfect. Everyone says so. Your mamma died. I am a prophet of Gwad, and I have the power to make her come alive. You will never know she died by the time I am done. Your rent is late. Do not wait, give me all your money so I can celebrate. I will bless you for doing that. God approves that. Tell your friends, tell your dad, if you don't tell them Gwad will be mad. Listen to me because all the power is in my hands."

His hand waived to his choir. The lights in the church went red, and all of their eyes looked like they were mesmerized by his movement. His tail knocked a chair away in front of her. "He is perfect, perfect, perfect! Do what he says or face the wrath of Gwad," the choir sang away. "Come here so I can eat you alive," he spoke. "You stood up against me? A prophet of Gwad, one so holy! I will make you look bad to everyone because you made me angry!" Fueled by her resistance, perhaps knowing his game was at a critical moment, he roared in anger.

She fell backward, shaking — the inward part of her strengthened. Almost like the Christ in her stood with her in the truth. She leveled her gaze and looked him in the eye, and said, "But you lie, you are a liar; God is not here with you. Satan, the Lord rebuke you" In an instant, her sword was in her hand, and she touched him on the head. The costume and shell of the man fell straight down to the ground. Then the whole thing pulsed as if it was taking a few giant breaths, and on an intake, the clothes and skin of the man burst and fell apart. His inwards, the blood, gut, and gristle, smelled as nasty as an old grave, and the stench of it stung her eyes. She coughed a little, bending forward, eyes tearing and gasping.

Out of the carnage, the snake arose. There was no soul there. This she was sure of; she was looking at her enemy face to face.

"I will give you my gold for your soul," it hissed, "come stand by me."

"Your gold is worthless in my eyes and the eyes of my God, the Creator."

She spits on the floor. "Get behind me, Satan. You have nothing to offer me."

The eyes of the snake flashed in dead anger and went to speak a manipulative lie again. Then part of her stood up. This thing was a liar; he did not serve her God. He was a pompous, deceptive thief. He wasn't holy. She needs to hear none of his words.

"The Lord rebuke you, Satan, be silent." Her sword glinted through the air. Suddenly his tongue was caught in a trap. She laughed as he could not speak another word. His tongue writhed on the floor. The lights stopped; the choir was silent. The snake fell like a worm to the floor.

She said, "I renounce every contract, any belief or agreement I ever had with you or any of your kind. I repent of ever believing in your lies, known or unknown. I declare that any agreement known or unknown we ever had is broken. I declare it in the name of Yeshua."

As she spoke aloud these words in this room, a golden light pushed out the neon. Everywhere the golden light touched a member of the congregation, the puppet chains fell off of them, and scales fell from their eyes. They turned into sheep without hair, sheared sheep with their bones showing starving for food. Those that were snakes fell and slithered on the floor.

She felt a mix of emotions within herself. She wished she had discerned who he was earlier. Normally she would feel a bit guilty, but as she watched this pompous charade come to a screeching halt, she saw exactly what she was dealing with. There was no return because there was no man there. She began to pray and called upon the arch angels to come and help clean this up.

Pity filled her heart when she saw the congregation. Broken, abused, and deceived. Her foot pushed the snake's fat body and said, "My dad's coming for you." Her heart smiled, "You ain't seen nothing yet."

The wind of the wings of 1,000 angels rushed in. The building began to buckle in on itself. The light showed in, and all the clothes of the remaining congregation disappeared, and they stood there naked and wretched.

One by one, the sheep in the congregation began to look at each other and weep. Without clothes, you could see that many were not even humans; they were snakes with human blood dripping from their mouths and wolves.

One of the walls glowed with golden light, and it opened, and the Good Shepard came to collect His missing sheep.

He stared at the men who worked for the snake, and their lives flashed before them. Each one had been given a ball of gold. They stared at it as they got older, the balls got bigger, and as the balls got bigger, they turned more and more into demons. They looked at the Shepard, completely demonized with balls of gold in their hands. "Was it worth it?" He asked. The angel of death swiped their heads off, and their bodies fell.

"It is time to leave my people; come out of here," the Shepard said to the sheep.

The good angels came to gather the flock. She was surrounded in light, three stars that were gifts of hers dislodged from the building, like stolen treasure, and spun towards her sparkling, and then the light was so great she was moved through space and time.

CHAPTER TWELVE

Sleeper Awaken

Sarah had just woken up and now could embrace the joy of it. She was a stranger on this earth, royalty belonging to a place far away, and she had almost forgotten who she was and what her inheritance was. She was of the kind that would always be a child, although some earthy years and experiences had collected. She was a dreamer with many gifts, all of which she could now begin to share.

Many humans seem to be sleeping, often caging themselves behind masks and running from their true feelings. Thinking the things that would save them or set them free were found outside of their hearts. They possessed much and hungered for more.

Foundations were the things that buildings stood upon; every mansion was built upon them. Every kingdom had them. She was rebuilding her entire house to get the foundation right. Building from the rubble. She had an opportunity to build right, creating a kingdom in truth that would not crumble.

She wasn't really sure about the exact moment in her life that she died. Or if it was a series of deaths over time. Did that matter anymore? She stopped herself from looking back. She drew her foot in a line on the floor, raised her arm over her head, and leaned back into the exhale. There was something to the music that played. Classical, brain music, they called it. No words, propaganda, self-abuse, or worldly destruction, just poetry in sound. Like as if nature and humans met and held hands.

Waking up from a dead life was probably as difficult as entering into a butterfly's chrysalis. Everything you know, everything you had hoped for, every lie you pretended was your reality destroyed themselves one by one. You went from crawling on the earth, driven by hunger, to drawing into yourself, splitting yourself open, and wrapping yourself in deep protection by hardening your outsides. All of you become liquid; your genes activate, and within yourself is some secret code that awakens you into your new life.

She danced to the cords of a cellist playing a melody by Bach. The last cord played, and she rested. As her chest breathed in and out, she cast a look into the fear, and her eyes met with what she once feared. Self-hate is a targeting advertising message. You are not good enough. Her core felt remarkably strong, though. The mirror could not shake her anymore. Her beauty had remained unbroken despite the lines she had acquired that spoke the stories of the last few years.

You know when you hold a mirror and try to see yourself, then realize you only have a fragment in your hands, like your soul had been somehow broken, and you need the pieces to see your reflection clearly. Sometimes we lose these pieces within us; it is funny how trauma can take us deep into places that are misaligned with the truth.

Part of waking up is the light becoming one with you, and each and every footstep can begin to help others see the way home.

Her sister, who was her friend a long time ago, was a dreamer; she had many gifts and a calling. Sometimes when we grow up among sleeping strangers, we learn to hide the gifts. To become smaller than we really are, we silence the truth every time we lose a part of ourselves. We can remember how to find our broken pieces. Then you can remember that you are a foreigner that lives in a strange world. Your soul is not from here; you come from another place.

Her sister was very tall. Very straight and rigid. Her wrist had an electronic band on it - the killers were trying to capture her forever. A raging wolf was trying to be her soul. He howled in the realms around her and eyed the girl with red eyes. The wolf shook with fear as the girl's eyes flashed with the light of all the universe within them. Christ in her stared back, and she heard the evil wolf whimper. Having an evil spirit assigned to you is a nasty thing. It will whisper lies into your ears and whisper lies into the ears of the people around you. Her hand gripped her sword, and in her mind's eye, she saw the dark wolf that craved the blood of her sister cut in half.

"Come with me, sister," she cried. "I saw you. I know where you are. Let's enter the kingdom." She ran and ran with her sister through the city streets. As they ran, the world shifted around them. Her sister's eyes grew wide as they went deeper into an alley of past time. Suddenly a yellow bricked road appeared and wound into the world. They were very deep in a suspended room of memories. She was here. Her sister. The splinter. She was just a few years old, standing in a beautiful pink ballet dress. She was alone in a dull, dark room of emptiness. The words had placed her there. Sometimes caretakers can say the cruelest things.

"This is part of you! You are here!" Her sister shook her head and said, "I have to be normal; I am Pandabjørn, she said automatically." She held her sister with great compassion. So many in this world try to conform to demonic rules even though, in their deepest heart, they know they are called to something greater. One life can change the planet.

Sarah had no fear of a dark wolf because Christ lived within her. She could see its strategy to try to keep her sister angry inside. She looked into her sister's eyes and said, "God loves you exactly how you are, Pandabjørn. You are good. He knows you like to play; dress up. It is safe for you to know and love this missing part of you." In her sister's mind's eye, she clearly saw the little girl wanting to dance in the ballerina dress. "Reconnect with your child, reconnect. She is pure and beautiful and a strong, powerful dancer; you can protect her. You can become the perfect mother to her. God can show you the way.

Her sister wrinkled her nose. "I have to be normal; I have forgotten." She shook the band of the dead on her wrist. The band of the bored. It clinked like chains of slavery.

"Hmmf." She touched her fingers to her sister's head and blew the breath of awakening at her. They both saw the ballet girl begin twirling and dancing and laughing. They grabbed hands and danced - twirling in a circle. The room's color changed to a bright sunny yellow. Windows appeared opening into the beautiful outdoors, and a group of birds landed on the windowsill and began singing.

They laughed even more.

Her sister held herself; she held her face in her hands, and with the light connected between their eyes, both smiled. The energy from her inner child who had fractured became one with her body. At the same moment, a howl of evil erupted, and a dark wolf shadow ripped from her body. There was no place for it to hide because the light filled her now. She stood smiling and shining, and the electronic bracelet broke off her wrist.

"What the heck was that?" She spoke. "Seriously." Her sister seemed more of herself than she ever had. The joy within her was solid.

"When your soul fractured as a child, it left an opening for the darkness to enter; now it has no place in you. The evil lies; all it does is come to steal, kill, and destroy your life." She wanted to share so much. "Remember, it feels a lot better to know you are loved than to think you are forgotten and alone. The Creator loves you so much... He showed me you were here."

"Get better and gear up. You are doing good, but how often do you know there is something more? You can have a sword and walk between the worlds. After all, we are not from here." She paused, and her eyes moved upward and then leveled with her sister's. "Everything is about to change; wake up, oh sleeper, and follow the way. Want to go dungeon hunting with me? We can steal back souls."

Little and her perfect timing snorted.

"You have never wanted to go dungeon hunting before."

CHAPTER THIRTEEN

The Dungeon

The mansion shifted rapidly, dropping down with the girl and her sister almost like an elevator. Poof, all of a sudden, all of the light seemed to disappear, and shadows played upon the walls. In front of her was a dark hallway; a neon light began to flicker on and off. It was written in English and in Hebrew. Red and blue neon and an arrow pointing downwards. "The dungeon" was written in both languages.

"Well, it looks as if we have found the dungeon." Little purred.

"It's fairly obvious." The girl's sister agreed. Little sat in front of the hallway staring at the girl, waiting for her next move. You could see the cat grin hidden right under a level of cat seriousness. Utterly cool in the moment before the face of danger.

"No, no, no, no, just no. I don't even want to go in there." The girl told Little. Perfectly calm and fluffy as usual, Little was in the midst of licking her paw. Cats always seem to do the most random things in some of the most inappropriate times.

Little stopped and looked at her, exposing her cat grin, and said — "But you have to. You need to go in and rescue the part of you that is in that dungeon." The girl kicked the ground hard and sat down. "I don't think this is very fun at all; in fact, this completely sucks," she resisted. Her eyes welled up with big tears again. Her sister snorted. She slapped her glasses on her face like a protective shield and gave a wry smile. "I am in. Let's do this."

Little laughed. "Let's do this. There is nothing to fear, and I imagine we will find a good piece of you here."

The girl shouted, frustrated, "Don't you think I need my shield first?"

Little sneezed with a slight snort. "I think you will find what you need on the way. Let's go."

The girl's sister looked at her incredulously and said, "What is your problem? Let's go. You already have a sword, and all I am coming in with is this pencil." She held up a Mitsubishi Hi–Uni Pencil, HB Japanese-made. She reached into her pocket, dug around a little bit, and held up a pink eraser. "I've got this Paper Mate Pink Pearl Eraser too. We're good. We got this." She was savvy enough and had the instant memory that she was not from here. That the battle did not belong to her but the Creature of the Heavens and the Earth. It was that kind of battle you just needed to show up to.

The air shook around them as if it wanted to scare them out of this place. Some random noises came from the area of descent, otherwise known as stairs.

Together they began to walk down.

This route to the dungeon stank; to get to it, one had to descend through a very narrow, dim hallway that smelled like cat piss, tears, and the feces of rotting bulls. Surprisingly, the only thing that looked even halfway decent were the steps down the hall itself. They had been polished infomercial clean and had that mall-like escalator roll to them.

It was an easy descent back into a place she never belonged. It took everything she had not to judge herself with hate walking down this hallway. Words and statements had been scrawled all over the walls.

"DO THIS; YOU ARE NOT GOOD ENOUGH. YOU CAN'T DO THIS." The prose of a narcissist. They always want to keep you doubting yourself — words designed to weaken your will and give in.

The words almost lifted off the walls as she walked past them and seemed to breathe. Like an unseen presence behind them wanted to push them into her reality. She walked and shook a little as they tried to cast their shadows into her heart. It took a deep connection with her father in heaven, a core resonance of the freedom of the way of the heart to make each step. She focused on her breath. The love within her grew brighter and brighter, and the writing on the dungeon's stairway faded, and the shadows became nothing; they could not touch her.

Her sister started laughing. "Is this what you put up with? You lived like this! This is ridiculous. You had a crush on an infomercial 4th-grade Hogwarts guy? Stop!"

Walking down these stairs, she realized she had followed the magician. The one who tricked her into thinking he was walking with the Creator of all that is. It was a sour note he spoke when he confessed; he was a sorcerer, the kind of man that would sign away his soul for a small bit of power, the false light that only illuminated fake paths. As she looked around herself, she could clearly see how false this path, his path was, and the death it could lead her into.

Little and her sister chuckled away. They began singing. Around their feet, little flowers were popping up as they both gleefully descended towards the dungeon. The girl kept thinking.

She was so empty then, still seeking someone to love her; she had ignored all the red flags and, most of all, the messages that her heart gave her from the very beginning. He was a common rat: the kind who preyed on weak women. She had almost killed herself, pretending she was weak. Giving away her gifts and power just to be insulted. Anyway, it did not matter anymore.

A flower hit her on the side of her head. Her cat laughed. The girl was pretty sure her sister had thrown it at her.

Her thoughts created her inner reality. Her new glasses caused the words to shift on the walls, and she saw the truth behind them: GASLIGHTING, DIVERTING, SEDUCTION, MANIPULATIVE LIES. The words he had spoken did not matter because the truth set her free. If she had listened to God better, she could have avoided all of this. She wanted to beat herself up mentally but quickly remembered the Way to Stay Positive

Don't look back
Seek the solution
Trust God

She took another step down the stairs which looked pretty average now. As she walked into what she had feared with courage, her fears seemed to melt away. The stairs still stank, and it was really not the kind of place most people would enjoy. Perhaps if you were a rat or a cockroach, you could find this place inviting; there were plenty of them here. She turned her head and raised her eyebrow at Little and her sister and said, "This is not where we live; let's turn this place inside out." Like the wise cat she was, Little seemed to smile in silence. Her sister spoke under her breath and rattled off a few sentences about her whole perspective on the situation you could not quite hear.

Finally, they reached the bottom. At the end of the stairs was a large black door with a penguin sitting atop it. She supposed a crow would look a bit more menacing. She questioned inside herself... "this was the man she gave her power to?" Etched in the door in shoddy children's scrawl were ancient, supposedly magical symbols but not well executed —

the type of magic that would cave back in on itself because it was just ego, deceit, and the dark.

Her sister just laughed.

As they approached, the door woke up. It was a large wooden and metal door, and a fat, grotesque face was right in the middle. The door opened its eyes; demons flickered inside them. "I want your money." The door's mouth appeared, licking sticky lips. It burped a gas, and the smell of seduction and deceit filled the stairwell. It burped again, and stale smoke wafted outward.

She was glad Yeshua gave her glasses months ago, gifting her with the clear site. Seeing things clearly in the spiritual realm really helped. She almost laughed now, remembering how she had taken the sorcerer as seriously as she possibly could pretend to, and seeing what he was made of... she sneezed; she smelled the smoke of the thief.

In an instant, her sword was in her hand. This was the sword of someone who was sent to destroy the works of the devil himself. This was a sword given to her by the Creator of the Universe, and after all, she was one of the creator's top ten favorite people to hang out with, including Moses and Abraham. Holding the sword, she changed her stance entirely. A cloak of fear fell from her shoulders, and she stood in the strength of God.

Her body flashed, connecting with all time and space as she moved quickly; the sword was the word of the Creator Himself. She arched the sword high and smashed it far harder than needed in the pattern of a cross on the door. The door, all the working of evil, all the witchcraft and sorcery shattered and burned in the light and flames of the sword.

"Satan, get behind me." She spoke. It was done. In her mind's eye in the distance, she felt everything this man had done return to him; she let it go. Only he could repent for his evil intentions and lies. She had prayed and given enough already. She let it go and walked into a once sealed dungeon; the light from her body and her sword lit the whole room. It was as if the whole room had caught fire; you could see glimpses of things burning up—spells, broken contracts, lies, etc.

The magician was already gone from the room. He was not there. His type is always in search of their next victim. Listen to your heart, her voice sang to all the children, be careful because these days, there are many who would not value you for your true worth, who would discard you easily and just want to take from you. They are lovers of themselves and care not about you. Do not give them an inch or an opening into your lives. They will prostitute your body and abuse your soul. It is better to stay single and become strong, so you see your value is so much more.

She looked down at her feet, and a thin stream of blood touched them. There she was, she found herself, the fracture, sitting there in the center of the room, eyes blindfolded. Little, her cat quickly ran and hopped on the fracture's lap in a full purr. She met herself and took the blindfold off; it looked like a mask. Underneath her eyes were soaked in blood, the blood was so great that there were pools beneath her feet.

"Hey, how's it going?" She asked herself. The fracture of herself that was bound in this room. The fractured self spoke, shaking: "I made a contract with him; I have to do everything he says so God will love me." "It was a mistake." "God doesn't listen to me anymore." Her eyes stared into her own eyes, and all of a sudden, a light glowed within the fracture's eyes. In one voice, they said together, "I don't listen to lies anymore. I break all contracts with this man and any others like him. The thief comes only to steal and kill and destroy; Jesus has come that we may have life and have it to the full."

Light flashed around all of them, and this room shattered and collapsed forever. Suddenly Yeshua was there; He spoke a blessing, "I am making a way where there was no way. Never again will your hard work be given to others, never again." As He spoke, Sarah's soul healed, and the two became one, her fractured part merging with her soul. In her being, she felt a giant taproot being pulled out of her being. The sickness itself left her as her fractured soul healed.

She saw another door; an ordinary door was there. It had been fixed into place by a magician's curse. The energetic magic swelled and broke. Insanity was the word. The letters lifted off of the door, powerless and broken; they fell to the earth. Dark magic, the darkness lifted off of her chest and slipped into nothingness. In the corner of her eye, she saw the symbols of the sorcerer fall to the ground, moved out of place, and broken.

There were deep lessons she learned there about the day and age we live in. That the lips of people could speak words while their hearts hide deep lies. It was a day and age to know and walk closely with the Creator because the thieves were present.

"Do I get my sword yet?" Her sister asked, standing by them. "I would like a really big one, like a samurai or maybe a cleaver… yeah, cleaver."

The girl told her sister the sword is alive; it is the living Word of the Creator. If I had my sword sharpened before I got stuck here, I would have known what the ancient texts had cautioned:

But understand this: In the last days, terrible times will come, for men will be lovers of themselves, lovers of money, boastful, arrogant, abusive, disobedient to their parents, ungrateful, unholy, unloving, unforgiving, slanderous, without self-control, brutal, without the love of good, traitorous, reckless, conceited, lovers of pleasure rather than lovers of God, having a form of godliness but denying its power. Turn away from such as these!

They are the kind who worm their way into households and captivate vulnerable women who are weighed down with sins and led astray by various passions, who are always learning but never able to come to a knowledge of the truth.
- Ancient Text Quote

"Yeah," she said. "Watch out for these narcissistic little rats. It is not your job to change them, just to discern who they are and leave them behind." She touched her sword in comfort. "The word makes sense; it is better than conforming to the lies of the world. I know I am created to be more than I have been."

She knew at this moment that they both would survive. A tear fell out of her eye in gratitude. As that tear fell, it joined the tear of Christ that fell the moment her soul had entered here, and the mercy of

God healed everything at that moment. The dungeon began crumbling around them. Lie upon lie withered and died, and the room lost all of its power. It became nothing. It was utterly destroyed, and she would never return to that place.

The worlds shook the room, and the walls collapsed.

Then they all were sitting in her beautiful house on her farm. Her heart filled with the light of Christ; the kingdom of God gained a space in her heart. At this moment, she had hope that they would do more than survive in the coming times.

CHAPTER FOURTEEN

The Conman

It was a new day. She had become a hunter now. She knew that there was something she needed to do. She was ready to collect her soul from those who deceived her. It was time to visit someone. She held up her sword, and the light of God surrounded her, and she flashed to a different place in time.

"I can cure you. I have the medicine." His fingers were stained the color of tobacco, and he smelled like smoke. When he spoke, it was like speaking to a magician. His words painted stories; his clothes painted him. Natural fabrics, a hat, a feather or two, and a leather pouch. He sat in front of her, and smiling, he opened his leather pouch and prepared a powdery substance which he put into an oddly etched hollow bone. "PHHHPT," he blew the substance now in the bone up into his own nose.

She watched him.

He shook a rattle at her head. Then he lit a cigarette and waved it in all directions, looking very serious. She stared at him smoking. She saw in the spiritual realms dead spirits coming to smoke his cigarette with him. "Let me tell you about the sacred tobacco. How it takes your prayers to heaven." She saw right next to him in the inter dimension a dead man that tried to smoke his cigarette with him. He went on and on about tobacco. About his long relationship, how he was holy, how he earned all the privilege, and how it protected him. Now there were three people smoking with him. One of the dead person's eyes grew wide as they saw her watching them.

Years ago, she was there with his type. Years ago, she believed him. They knew how to vomit. Deep within the Amazon jungle, they drank the brews of the plants there. Years ago, she did not have glasses. He was a con man, posing as a path to God, a spiritual drug peddler. What he wanted was control. Now she wanted her soul.

She breathed in and out as she watched the heavens. Three death angels moved like missiles through the night sky. They were tracking her. Things happen in the jungles. She challenged the conman. A con artist peddler of special plants, money for the experience. She closed her eyes, thanking the Creator for the mercy He shed upon her life.

She started praying to the Creator to come. The conman shaman was angry with her. She knew the truth, and she had caught him in lies. Isn't it amazing how predators get so angry when you see their lies? She did not care. She did not need his tainted medicine; she needed the blessing of the Creator of life. She began asking God to show her the way.

As she prayed, she saw the faces of the painted men in the jungle, evil alters, bones, and chicken blood right on the other side of tourism. "Dear Heavenly Father, I was deceived. Please forgive me for Pharmacia, please forgive me for witchcraft, for practicing magic whether I knew about it or not. Please break every covenant, agreement, evil alter, anything I know of or not know of that happened during those times."

One of the death angel birds crashed from the sky, and at the same moment, she saw an altar breaking behind a fire. It exploded in front of drumming men. "Dear God, I renounce any soul ties, any contracts I made with any spirits, people, or entities using medicine."

Another death angel bird crashed to the ground as a cord around her wrist with the conman loosed and came off of her. She coughed up a bone and watched the power of an alter with chicken blood break. A huge heaviness left her back with the conman's energy, "I hate you."

"Dear God, please restore me to your Kingdom, your path, and let me come home. I renounce this path." The third death angel bird fell, and a giant eye appeared in the Sky and crashed and burned. A finger pointing at her broke off.

She lit a match and stood before a fire she had made ready. Every object of her past connection that she could find was piled on top of some wood. She tossed the match upon a pile of dry kindle and watched it flicker and catch fire. She had soaked some gas on everything, and flames quickly consumed the pile. Books, feathers, clothes, she burned it all.

In her mind's eye, she saw a piece of her broken self trapped in a small metal subterranean sealed box; the words of the conman had sealed it with cords as the fire burned the cords burned around the box. As they dissolved in the fire, they screamed, "I Am Alone." The box broke open, releasing the girl's fracture.

"You are not alone she said to the broken piece of her. You are not alone!" She repeated. An anaconda snake came out of the metal box, the conman's trap. It slithered up a brick chimney. The stone gargoyle perched at the top came to life and moved. The snake's face appeared at the top of the chimney and wretched and shook as it vomited out a bright star and then the small fracture of the girl's soul into the night sky. The stones of the chimney broke apart and formed a barrier.

The fracture stared at the girl with golden eyes and a dark body. She was silent. The girl started saying, "I plead the blood of Jesus." The sky moved, and the universe shifted. The golden-eyed fracture of her soul turned to pure warm light and entered the eyes of the little girl. Everything shifted to positive. God spoke:

"I will make you into a great nation,
and I will bless you.
I will make your name great,
and you will be a blessing.
I will bless those who bless you,
and whoever curses you, I will curse,
and all peoples on earth
will be blessed through you."

"Sex and cigarettes," she said. They attract the dead. Both things need to be mastered. Repent for the Kingdom of Heaven is here. She hugged herself because repenting was pretty much super cool. She thought about all of these people, acting so hip, saying how love was the only answer, that everything was so cool. How many of them shriek when you say the name Jesus? How many of them condemn the

Dao, the path of Christ? Conmen, beware of those who come to you in sheep's clothing but are ravenous wolves inside.

In stillness, her soul willed to let this past go. In her heart, she prayed to never be conned again. She repented for her involvement in witchcraft. A huge weight on her back lifted off, and heavy snakes revealed themselves and then were ripped out of the air around her. She was free and felt lighter than she had in quite some time.

Reality flashed, and they were outside of the dead building. A giant hand appeared and lifted and crewed her up, and suddenly they all stared up at the forlorn building they had been running around in.

God spoke. "It is time to get rid of this."

"Let's do this," God spoke.

The fingers snapped against the building, and it immediately began to fall, crashing down upon itself, everything in it, and everything it represented. They all watched in silence as the building completely disappeared, and the ashes fell to the ground in front of their feet and dissolved into nothingness. Every last bit of grayness and concrete was gone. Like a paintbrush sweeping across reality, this space became a vast area filled with lightness and joy.

The girl knew that the kingdom she had created inside herself had been trapped in the lower realms, and now she knew the hell within her was completely destroyed. A great flash of light appeared over the area, a fire burned, and the world shifted around her. In the golden flash of the fire, she returned to a garden.

Now that you have descended, it is time to come back up.

CHAPTER FIFTEEN

Rest

Then she was there, resting. She was quiet after the battle. After battles are good, it is like a down winding, a time for healing, a need for deep care, a time of rebuilding. She leaned back against the most gorgeous tree. She appreciated the feel of the bark against her back. She felt the life in the tree, the life in God's creation, the Mother Earth beneath her feet. Her senses were attuned to the sound of the bees, butterflies, and dragonflies around her. She saw an inchworm making its way up a flower stem. She was wearing a necklace of teeny lilac flower petals.

"Good to see you, princess, you look brighter and lighter." The inchworm made its way into the center of the flower, the flower had a deep yellow hue, and the sacred geometry of its design was an echo, part of the divine heartbeat. It was a royal inchworm, a very special inchworm in the kingdom of inchworms; it worked directly with the creator. The inchworm sipped some dew from the center of the flower. "The morning dew is the best, quite restorative, very refreshing."

The inchworm smiled a while, its eyes new and green as the greenest plant. It was dappled in pink dots across its back. "Princess, may this day grant you wisdom and heal your heart to beat as one with the Creator. May no man step in between you again and separate you from the truth inside. Many seek the way of heaven; many long to know the truth, few can find it through the heart called and chosen you are, called and chosen." Seven ladybugs flew up and joined the inch worm on the flower. They began singing a song of worship:

Holy is the creator of life.
Holy are the gifts and wisdom you share!
Holy is your gift of life.
You are Holy!

The animals and creatures of the forest joined in the song; the bunny came, and the deer and Little played with the butterfly. The little girl rested, and the Creator put his hand on her forehead and said, "You did a good job."

She sat thinking, where do we go from here?

Just then, Christ appeared in the interdimensions; with a movement of His hand, she was clothed in a white wedding dress. As the dress shifted through the dimensions, it changed into the highest technological armor she could ever imagine. It became one with her, perfectly attuned to her being. The helmet connected her with the mind of Christ; in front of her eyes appeared a dimensional screen, and she saw things that she had never perceived before.

The armor molded over her ears, and suddenly she was attuned to the highest vibrations. She felt an incredible peace wash over her. In front of her mouth, her voice was ported through the God field, and she spoke in divine authority. She fell upon one knee in reverence and gratitude. The dress shined golden and spun around her skin, aligning with every energy point in her body. As the armor formed, anything left that was not in alignment, even the smallest chain, broke off. The armor sealed her flesh, and her energetic field was as soft as silk yet was otherworldly, like the armor of an angel. Nothing could penetrate it. As it covered her back, a mark came off of the center; the enemy had marked her with a symbol for people to be angry with her; never again could it take hold. The armor grew and surrounded her body, shielding it in divine truth.

Nothing, no man, spirit, or angle dimension, could separate her from God's blessing and protection. As it moved up her chest, a huge sludge came off. She stood in the strength of the Creator. She saw her youth restored and the many things that were to happen. Her exhale was great. In this armor, she felt close to home.

As the armor continued to form with her body, her entire spiritual being was drawn into alignment with the Creator. Destruction was cast far from her.

The rainbow rose up from the inside of her and surrounded her skin; her eyes glinted with the electricity of eternity. Her heartbeat was in step with time; it was the absolute love of the universe in perfect step with the love God had for her. As she smiled, the aura of the creator surrounded her. She stood in goodness; she stood in grace. She stood freed.

The Creator smiled on her life and lifted her up in goodness. Simple was her heart, quiet was her heart, and kind was her mind. She became gentle first towards herself, and it reflected outward towards all living beings.

She had climbed a great mountain to get here, and now she rested.

What is within you, they can never take from you

Introduction

For years, she knew she was supposed to write a book. She asked God often, with tears in her eyes, for the perfect words.

Then one night, a dream came to her.

Words were written in that dream:
Why not start with this?
I am the God of Moses, Isaac, and Jacob.
I am your friend.

I am your friend; The Great I Am repeated.
I am not a monster. You created the monster.

Those without sin cast the first stone,
Without judgment, this includes yourself.
My only religion is Mercy.
I am; you are

The Creator of Heaven and Earth, the Great Spirit, came to her and said

> *"It is time; it is time now to get your foundation right.*
> *Break down the walls of sorrow, breakdown the walls.*
> *Transform. Break down the walls, the boundaries."*

The kingdom of heaven is here already. The kingdom of heaven is within us. It is time to restore the kingdom.

There are some things they want the children to forget, to become blind to, to lose touch with. They want to change the children, control them, their minds, their beliefs, and sometimes their comings and goings. They are the wolves clothed like sheep and snakes clothed in human skin. If you open your eyes, you can see them, but you must awaken and unlearn The Forget.

All of us have been called to a path we can follow. You can't just go looking for it outside of yourself. It is the kind of path that reveals itself as it is being walked upon. If you get the combination right in your heart, it is the type of path that opens up right in front of you. It is a path that is living. It has no set direction, led by the gentle whispers in the wind. There is a certain kind of love that illuminates this path, something sacred. It is the way of Yeshua, the Christ. The Dao. The first principle is that the way of Heaven is the way of the heart.

She was resting by the side of the path. At this moment, she found herself staring out at a beautiful expanse where she could see in almost every direction — gazing far ahead and far behind. Everywhere she looked, the scenery was vibrantly colored. The breathtaking vista, the greenness of the grass, the blue skies that hugged and kissed the earth, causing flowers to grow everywhere, the clouds and the trees which offered shade, and the rocks that dotted the landscape like little people resting here and there.

The butterflies dusted the air, and the birds sang to each other, creating a great symphony. The bees hummed, and the beetles played in the dirt. The girl was wonderfully happy. Her little cat was having a deep conversation with a small white mouse. They were quite engaged, sitting on rocks that reminded her of chairs and tables. A waterfall danced down a mountain behind them.

The girl leaned back on the earth and let the blades of grass tickle her body. She felt free, expansive, and absolutely in love with all there was. The butterfly that landed on her smiled, kissed her nose, then darted off into the sky, saying,

"I do wish the unicorn was here right now. I most certainly would like to speak to her today."

Oh, wait... This book did not start that way but hold on because it will lead us there.

The Work - Author's Note

Those of us that have come out of abusive and traumatic childhood experiences sometimes use those experiences to shape our consciousness of what love means. The cycle begins when we are taught to associate the feelings brought on by the trauma with the feeling of love. We continue to feed these traumas to ourselves and in our future relationships, creating a desperate cycle that leaves us continually feeling hurt, betrayed, and untrusting the potential goodness and kindness in others and ourselves. There is a way to break this cycle and step into the light and connect with the source of all goodness, with the Creator of all that is.

How to do this is buried deep within all of us. Things around us may spin stories suggesting that what we seek is somewhere outside of us, but healing and transformation need to occur deep within our souls. We must find the unsettled places within us and pour love, and true love into ourselves, saturating every part until it reaches the dark places that are hiding in the trauma, opening ourselves up to the trust, the love, and the light of the Creator. These gentle acts of kindness and care we give to ourselves will completely change our lives.

At the moment the trauma is occurring, before we can consciously register its effects, we stop breathing, almost as a reflex. I believe this moment of breathlessness allows us to store the pain of the trauma within us. I have often thought about how interesting it is that one of the holiest names of the Creator translates to the words "LIFE BREATH." It was a name that long ago was spoken a few times a year and only by a priest because of its sacredness.

Ancient texts, like the Bible, speak of our human race being created from the earth and brought to life by the breath of God. I have found that when fractures of our soul are lodged in a trauma deep inside ourselves, we can use our breath and the presence of the Creator to release them.

Love is self-acceptance, forgiveness, and mercy; it is the salve for these traumatic wounds, and it is an experience of the light and power of Christ.

Love; its feeling is like a gentle smile. A kind of lightness that holds absolutely no judgment. It feels like freedom and acceptance. It is the embodiment of goodness. It goes beyond what our earthly fathers and mothers can give us and shifts the consciousness to our divine parents, the male, and female of the eternal Creator. It is within this space we can transform even the darkest imaginations and troubles into light, experiencing the miracle of how everything can shift. It is possible to make this transformation just by loving yourself and opening yourself to divine grace and mercy.

When traumatized, it is as if our energetic fields are unstable and unprotected. The brokenness of the spirit is having soul fractures and deep wounds. In these wounds, darkness is attracted to creating instability within our lives and experiences. To heal these wounds is to bring strength and wholeness to your entire being, which in turn, shifts the world around you and your experience of life. The people you were once attracted to, the things you found interesting, all the results of your exposures to these unhealed cycles will cease, and your life will change. Your feet will begin to steadily connect you to a path that leads you into the ways of life and understanding. Your old ways of doubt and pain will shift, and the space opened up within you will become a new place to rejoice within, and your heart will resurface. This is the work.

Facing yourself and identifying when and where these traumas have separated you is our work, your work. We have two choices, we can face ourselves and embrace ourselves and heal the traumas that cause these cycles to repeat, or we can repeat them. The work will feel hard because we must discard our feelings of being a victim and loneliness and face our fears. Doing this cultivates courage; in this courage, we cultivate compassion towards ourselves, allowing us to reflect ourselves authentically onto those around us. Echoing the deep love which embodies wisdom and lifts our hearts to kiss the heavens in a state of divine adoration and worship, showering this great outpouring of beauty into our lives and those around us. It is our true nature to become like a child again, or the child we knew we were, back in step with the divine blueprint.

Love first came to me in the dream state. Until this dream, I had no concept of the divine feeling of love. Love to me was horrible, angry, and abrasive, and it allowed no mistakes. This love was a reflection of the love I had been taught. It was utterly askew. In this dream, a voice said to me, "Try this love," and instantly, everything shifted. What I felt was the most beautiful feeling I had ever experienced in my life: everything was kind, no judgment, just being held in this pure, beautiful place of perfect comfort and care. That dream changed my life. It opened my eyes to a place where I wanted to be.

The work started when I woke up. I would imagine this love emanating through my hands, and I would touch my body, feeling the energy within me. Back then, my being was in need of great love. It was full of tangles, wounds, cords, and things I did not know how to let go of. Moment by moment, day by day, year by year, I started holding myself in this space of love.

Each morning, I would open myself to this love, and when I found a tension or a pain that did not match the energy I felt in the dream, I would hold it in this space of love. Going into this pain would cause emotions, old things, imaginations, and traumas, to surface. Breathing gently and just continuing to hold myself in love even there, without judgment, not engaging with the pain, just shifting this pain to a place of self-acceptance and love, I would feel the pain release and heal literally in my hands. I could hear the whispers of the injuries releasing, like the thoughts that bound the energies into place or the projections that I had stored from others.

The beginning of this work started me on a path that has brought me to where I am now. I am in a completely different space. I am in a completely different life. My life had been plagued by self-hate, and I was on a path seeking the destruction of my being and barely standing in the world. I was hurt so badly that I could not let anyone touch me. The Creator saw the pain that was hidden in my heart, and great mercy enabled me to be touched and transformed.

During this transformation, every step, every move, and every new experience took me on a journey that was nothing short of miraculous. During this journey, I became a woman who walks and trusts God in a divinely intimate way. Taught by the Creator personally and loved personally.

Coming to know that I am the electricity in every way can be expressed. My vibration is a subtle unique song authored by the Creator and whispered by me. I have come to face it and understand its innermost corners, yet still so unique; the experience continues to unfold.

A long time ago, I never stopped to listen to myself. My senses were teased, seduced, and bombarded by everything external. Eat me, touch me, be me, and be happy. Achievement, the external experience, promised a never-ending myth of fulfillment that left me oddly empty and unknown.

My anchors to life were tied to the things outside of me. The way I experienced them was through the stories I told myself. Many were echoes of pain and emotional discord. Although many would say I was fine, I knew I was not well. As dull as my ears were, I could perceive that inwardly I was filled with deep pain as if I was screaming.

Many of us know that we feel this way, but we are so unconscious of ourselves that we lack any skills to fundamentally make a difference. Solutions that treat the surface expression of the trauma are unproductive. Dismissing these feelings with drinks and company that yearn to escape themselves, seeking solace in smoking, pills, and anything that can shut off the pain for just a little bit only masks the true cause of the pain.

The bravest thing and, at first, the most painful thing I have ever done in my life is to face myself. To know and understand who I am and why I feel the way I do. To channel the deepest parts of my expression of pain into something profound and meaningful so that when I look behind me, it will make sense to others, and when I look within, I will know that is what my life came here to give. The first step to deeply loving myself began in a hug. I wrapped myself in a smile and went to meet me.

With Love,
Sarah